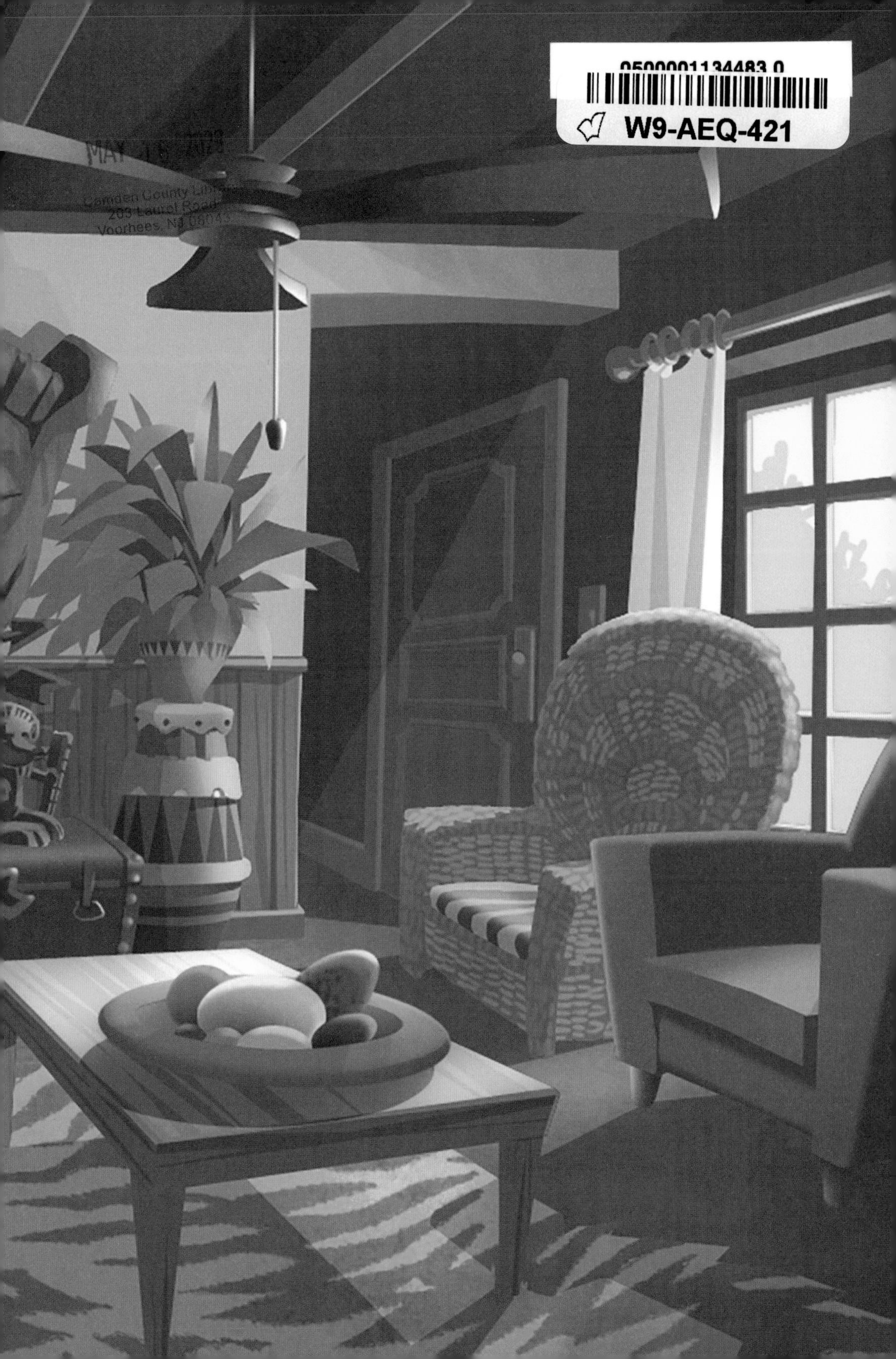

Geronimo Stilton™ Reporter

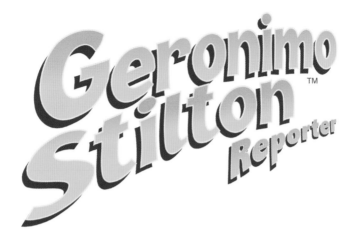

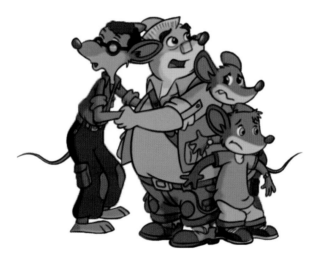

PAPERCUTZ

GRAPHIC NOVELS AVAILABLE FROM

PAPERCUTZ

GERONIMO
STILTON REPORTER #1
"Operation ShuFongfong"

GERONIMO
STILTON REPORTER #2
"It's My Scoop"

GERONIMO
STILTON REPORTER #3
"Stop Acting Around"

GERONIMO
STILTON REPORTER #4
"The Mummy with No
Name"

GERONIMO
STILTON REPORTER #5
"Barry the Moustache"

GERONIMO
STILTON REPORTER #6
"Paws Off, Cheddarface!"

GERONIMO
STILTON REPORTER #7
"Going Down to Chinatown"

GERONIMO
STILTON REPORTER #8
"Hypno-Tick Tock"

GERONIMO
STILTON REPORTER #9
"Mask of the Rat-Jitsu"

GERONIMO
STILTON REPORTER #10
"Blackrat's Treasure"

COMING SOON

GERONIMO
STILTON REPORTER #11
"Intrigue on the Rodent
Express"

GERONIMO
STILTON REPORTER #12
"Mouse House of the
Future"

GERONIMO
STILTON REPORTER #13
"Reported Missing"

GERONIMO
STILTON REPORTER #14
"The Gem Gang"

GERONIMO
STILTON REPORTER 3in1
#1

...ALSO AVAILABLE WHEREVER E-BOOKS ARE SOLD!

See more at papercutz.com

Geronimo Stilton™ Reporter

#13 REPORTED MISSING
By Geronimo Stilton

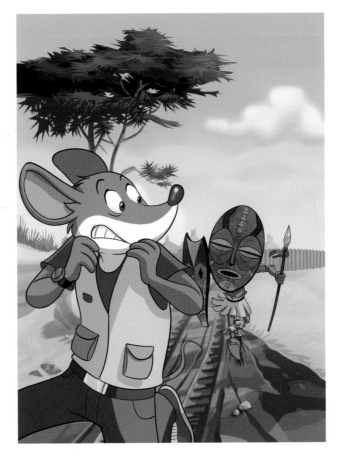

NEW YORK

REPORTED MISSING
Geronimo Stilton names, characters and related indicia are copyright, trademark and exclusive license of Atlantyca S.p.A.
All right reserved.
The moral right of the author has been asserted.

Text by GERONIMO STILTON
Cover by ALESSANDRO MUSCILLO (artist) and CHRISTIAN ALIPRANDI (colorist)
Editorial supervision by ALESSANDRA BERELLO (Atlantyca S.p.A.)
Editing by ANITA DENTI (Atlantyca S.p.A.)
Script by DARIO SICCHIO
Art by ALESSANDRO MUSCILLO
Color by CHRISTIAN ALIPRANDI
Original Lettering by MARIA LETIZIA MIRABELLA

Special thanks to CARMEN CASTILLO

TM & © Atlantyca S.p.A. Animated Series © 2010 Atlantyca S.p.A.– All Rights Reserved
International Rights © Atlantyca S.p.A., Corso Magenta, 60/62 - 20123 Milano - Italia - foreignrights@atlantyca.it - www.atlantyca.com
Published by Mad Cave Studios and Papercutz.
www.papercutz.com

Based on episode 13 of the Geronimo Stilton animated series "Geronimo, missione Africa!," ["Reported Missing"] written by CATHERINE
CUENCA & PATRICK REGNARD, storyboard by PIER DI GIÀ, LISA ARIOLI & PATRIZIA NASI
Preview based on episode 14 of the Geronimo Stilton animated series "La Rattobanda," ["The Gem Gang"] written by ANNETTA ZUCCHI,
storyboard by JEAN TEXIER

www.geronimostilton.com

Stilton is the name of a famous English cheese. It is a registered trademark of the Stilton Cheesemakers' Association.
For more information go to www.stiltoncheese.co.uk

JAYJAY JACKSON — Production
WILSON RAMOS JR. — Lettering
RACHEL WEISZ — Editorial Intern
INGRID RIOS — Editor
STEPHANIE BROOKS — Assistant Editor
REX OGLE - Editorial Director
JIM SALICRUP
Editor-in-Chief

ISBN: 978-1-5458-1025-5

Printed in China
February 2023

First Papercutz Printing

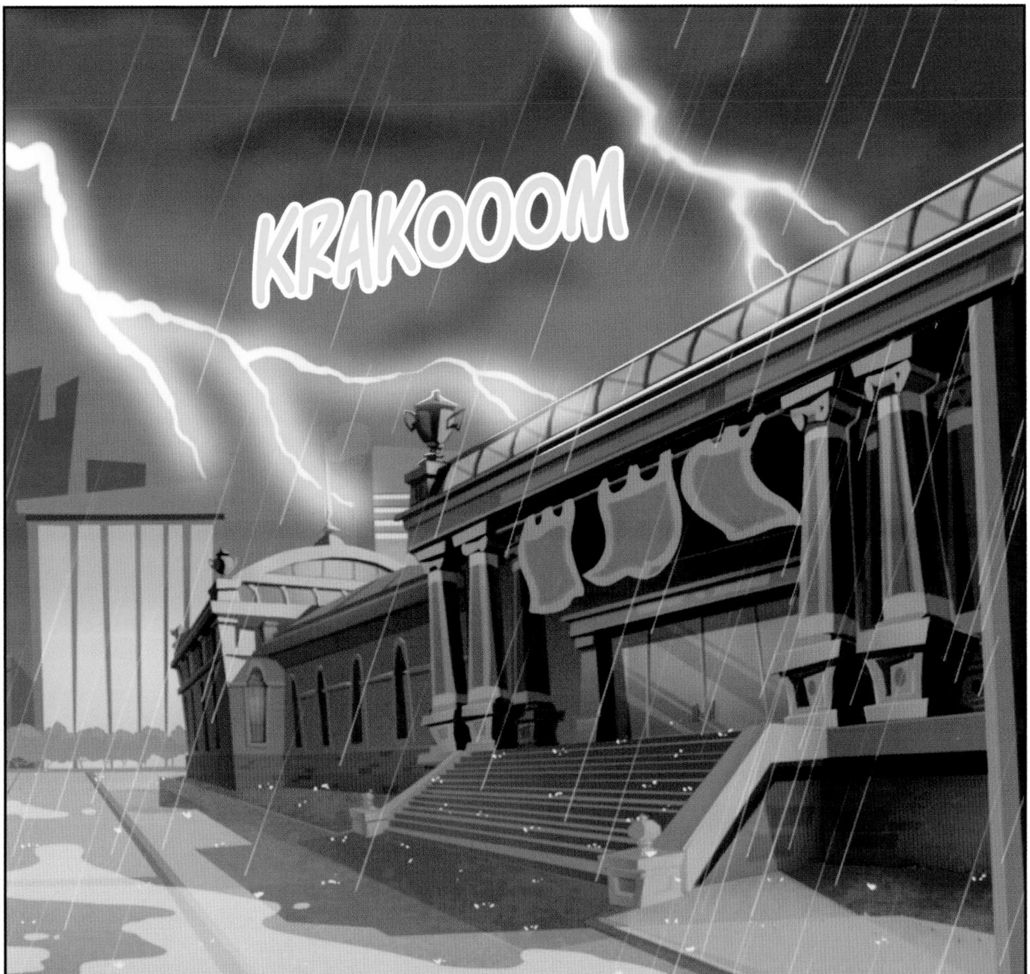
KRAKOOOM

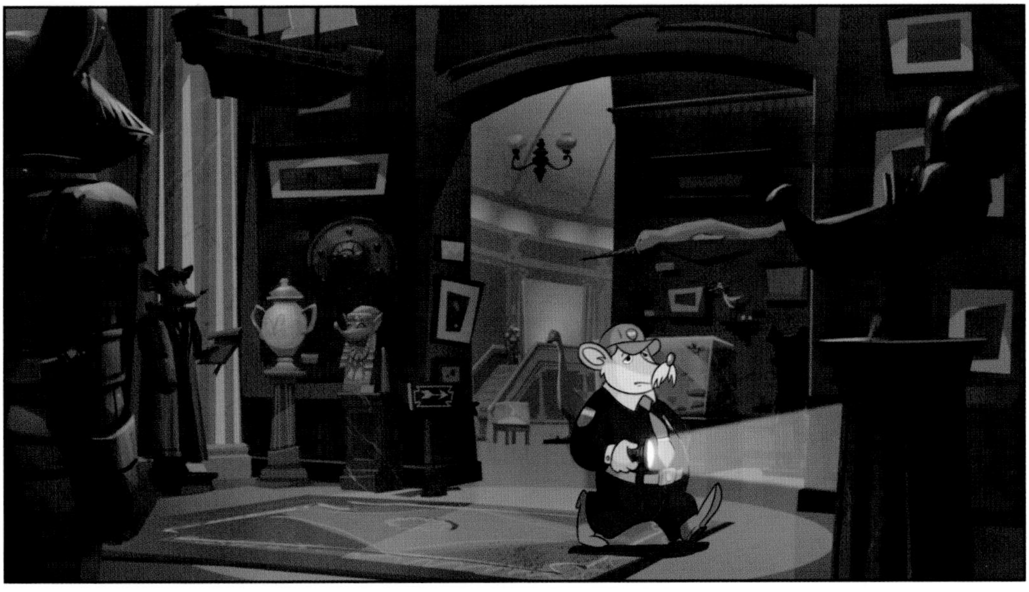

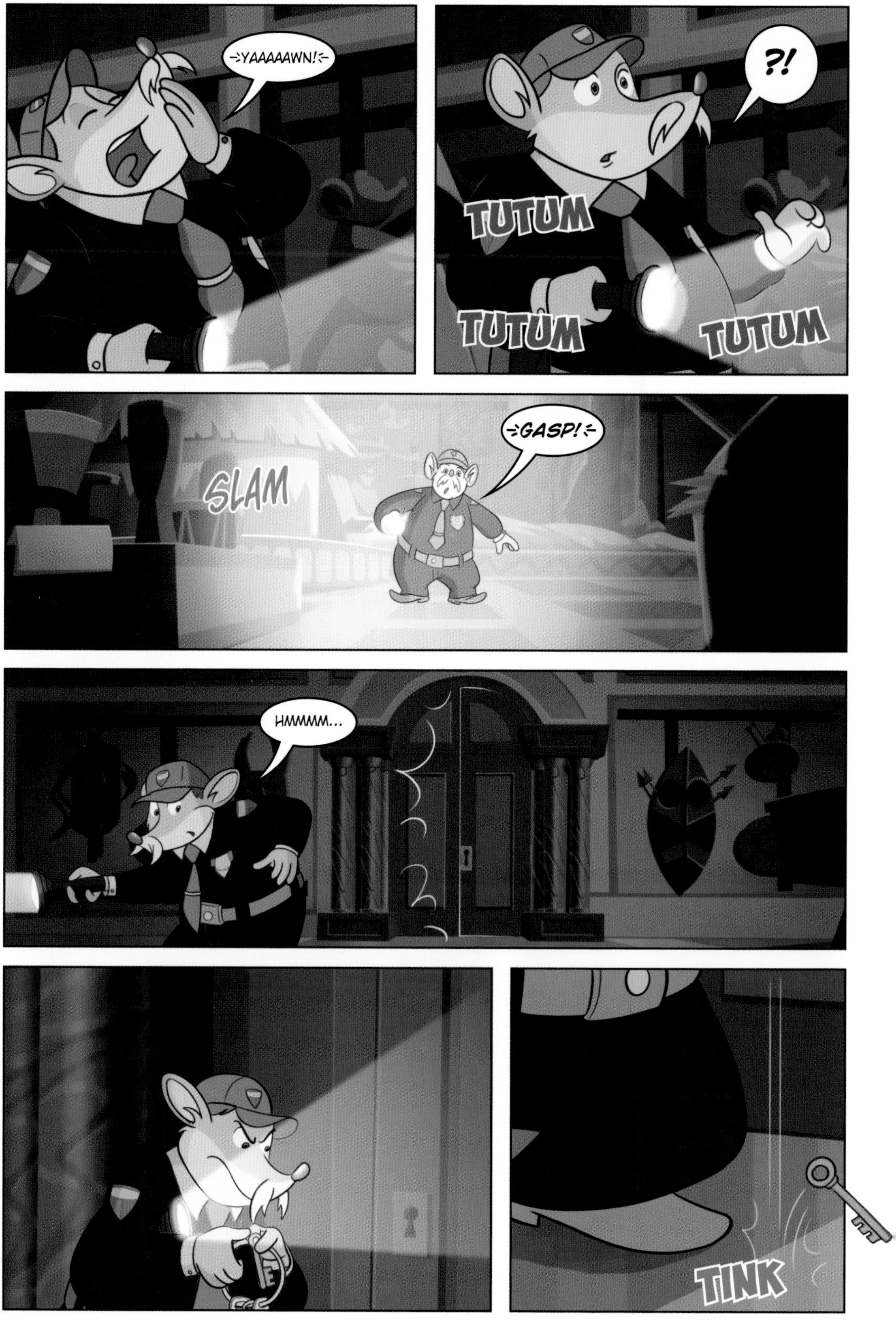

YAAAAAWN!
?!
TUTUM
TUTUM
TUTUM
GASP!
SLAM
HMMMM...
TINK

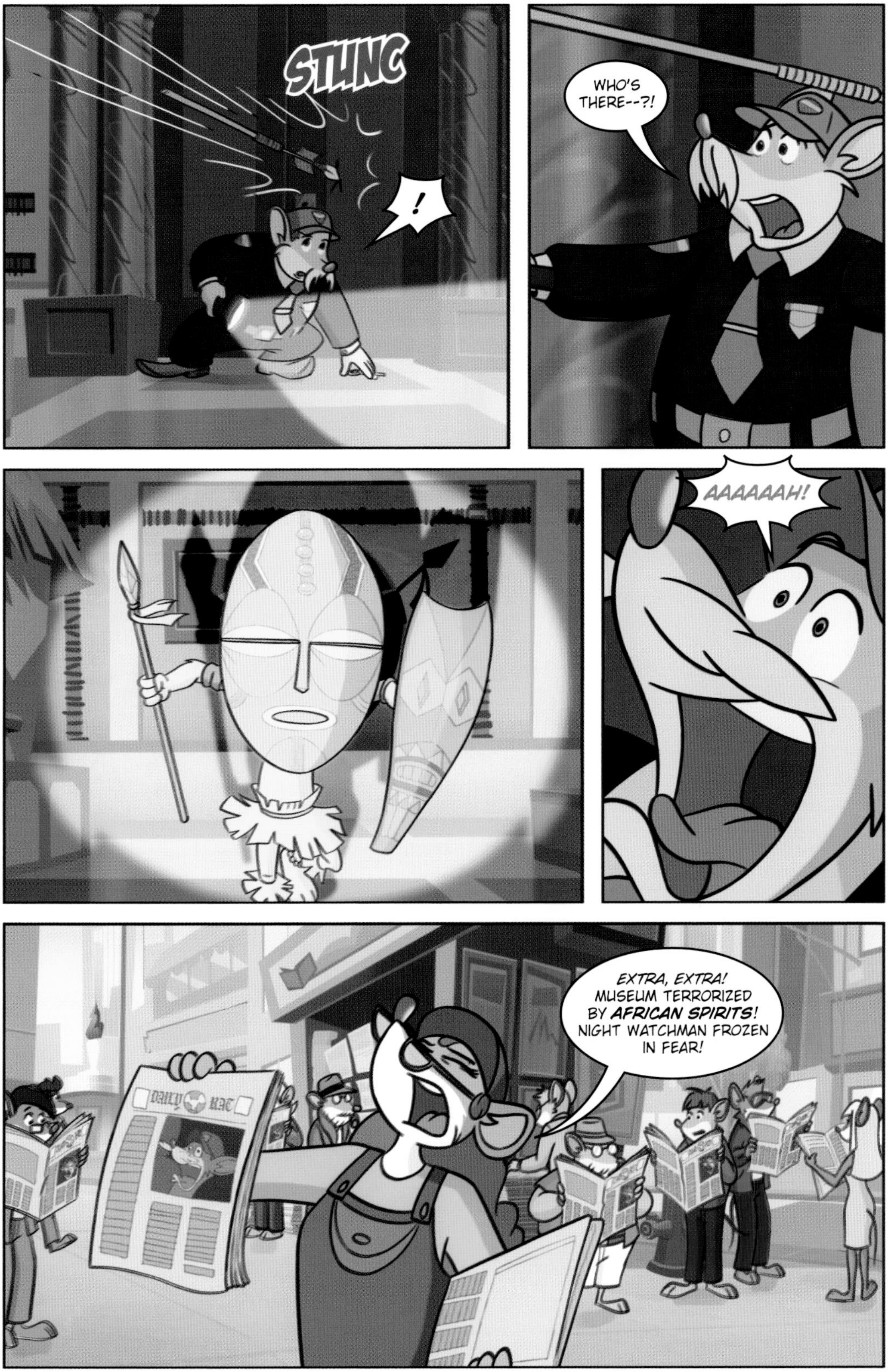
STUNC
!
WHO'S THERE--?!
AAAAAAH!
EXTRA, EXTRA! MUSEUM TERRORIZED BY **AFRICAN SPIRITS**! NIGHT WATCHMAN FROZEN IN FEAR!

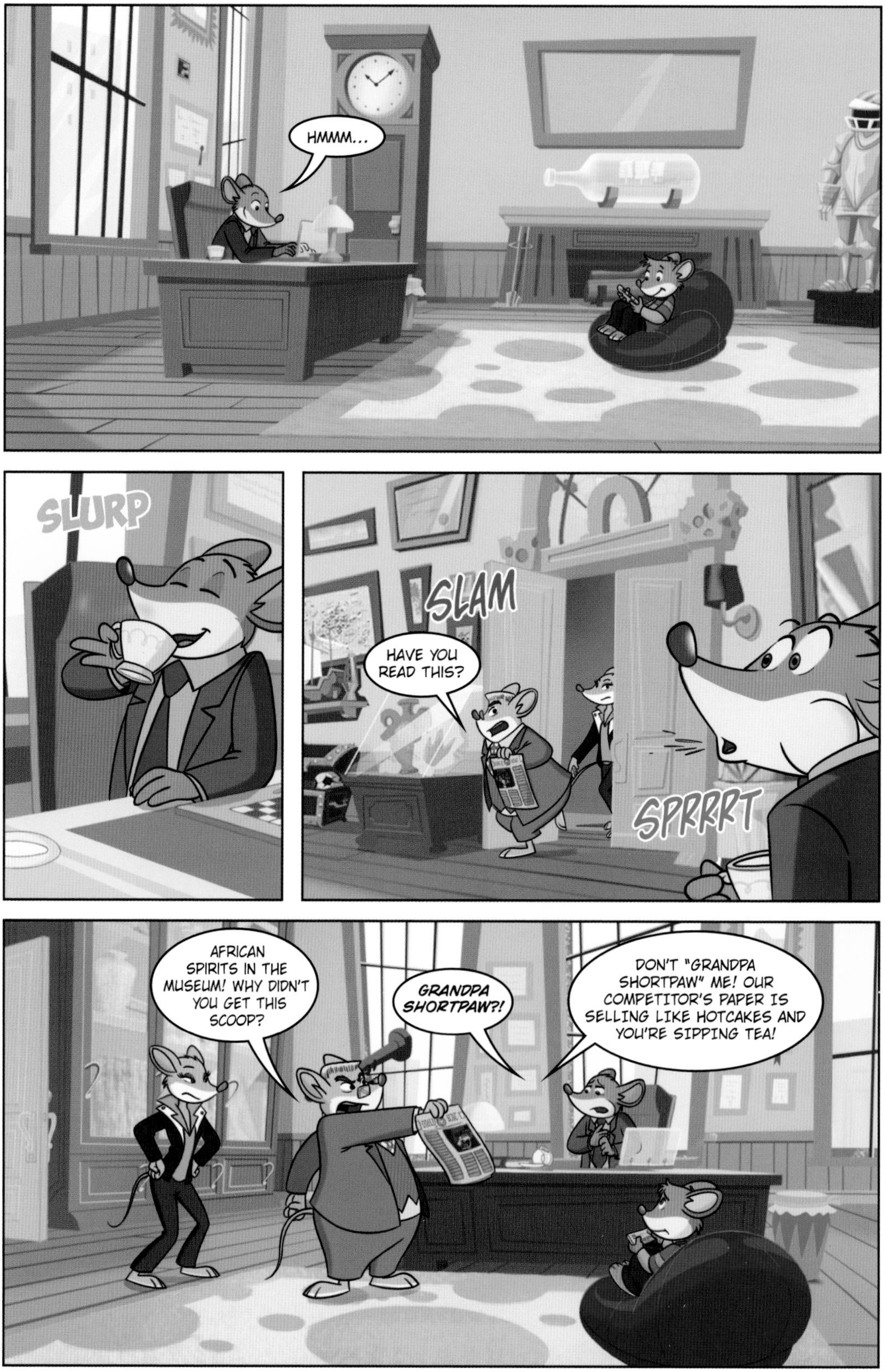
HMMM...
SLURP
SLAM
HAVE YOU READ THIS?
SPRRRT
AFRICAN SPIRITS IN THE MUSEUM! WHY DIDN'T YOU GET THIS SCOOP?
GRANDPA SHORTPAW?!
DON'T "GRANDPA SHORTPAW" ME! OUR COMPETITOR'S PAPER IS SELLING LIKE HOTCAKES AND YOU'RE SIPPING TEA!

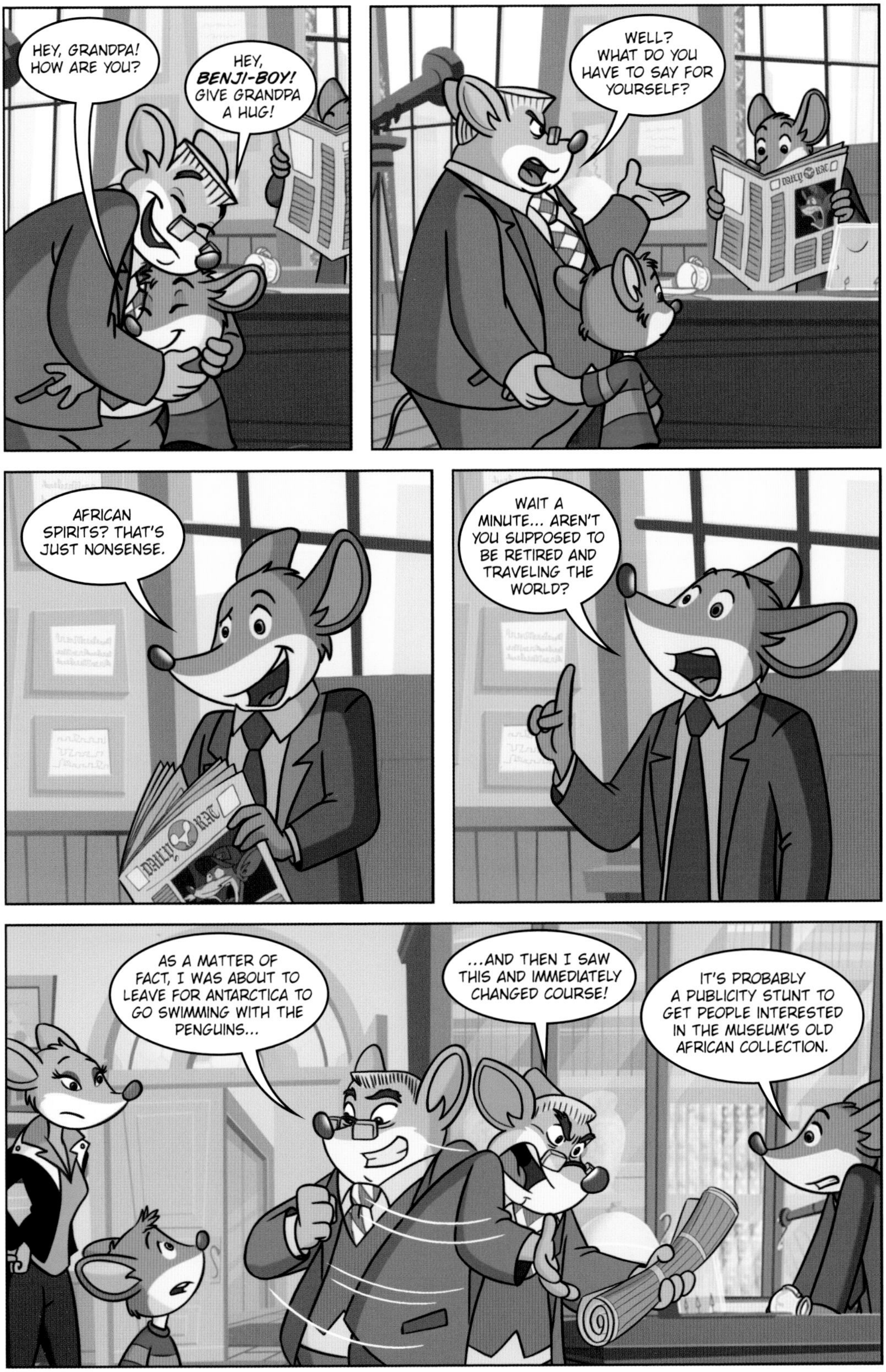
HEY, GRANDPA! HOW ARE YOU?
HEY, ***BENJI-BOY!*** GIVE GRANDPA A HUG!
WELL? WHAT DO YOU HAVE TO SAY FOR YOURSELF?
AFRICAN SPIRITS? THAT'S JUST NONSENSE.
WAIT A MINUTE... AREN'T YOU SUPPOSED TO BE RETIRED AND TRAVELING THE WORLD?
AS A MATTER OF FACT, I WAS ABOUT TO LEAVE FOR ANTARCTICA TO GO SWIMMING WITH THE PENGUINS...
...AND THEN I SAW THIS AND IMMEDIATELY CHANGED COURSE!
IT'S PROBABLY A PUBLICITY STUNT TO GET PEOPLE INTERESTED IN THE MUSEUM'S OLD AFRICAN COLLECTION.

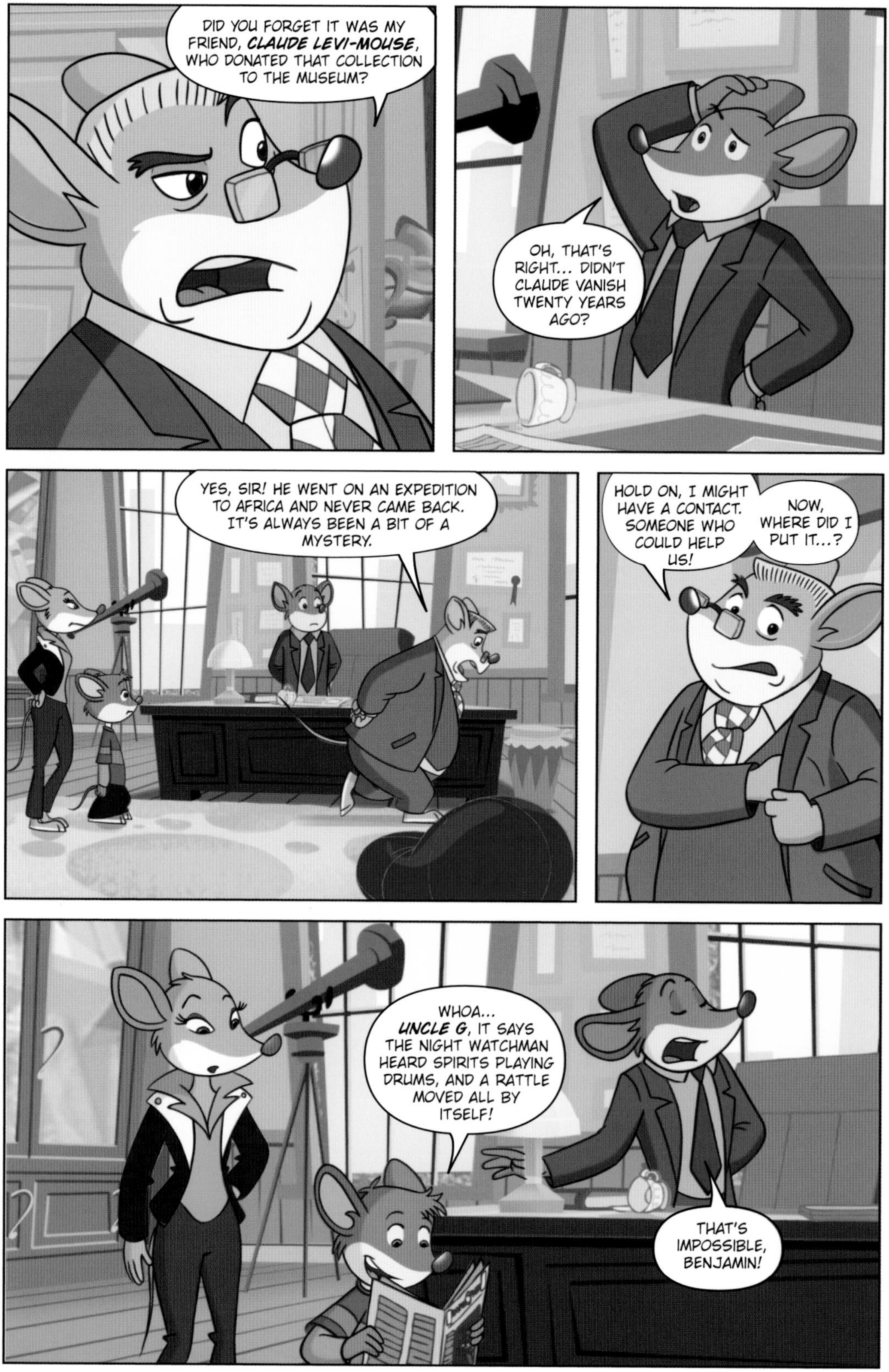
DID YOU FORGET IT WAS MY FRIEND, CLAUDE LEVI-MOUSE, WHO DONATED THAT COLLECTION TO THE MUSEUM?
OH, THAT'S RIGHT... DIDN'T CLAUDE VANISH TWENTY YEARS AGO?
YES, SIR! HE WENT ON AN EXPEDITION TO AFRICA AND NEVER CAME BACK. IT'S ALWAYS BEEN A BIT OF A MYSTERY.
HOLD ON, I MIGHT HAVE A CONTACT. SOMEONE WHO COULD HELP US!
NOW, WHERE DID I PUT IT...?
WHOA... UNCLE G, IT SAYS THE NIGHT WATCHMAN HEARD SPIRITS PLAYING DRUMS, AND A RATTLE MOVED ALL BY ITSELF!
THAT'S IMPOSSIBLE, BENJAMIN!

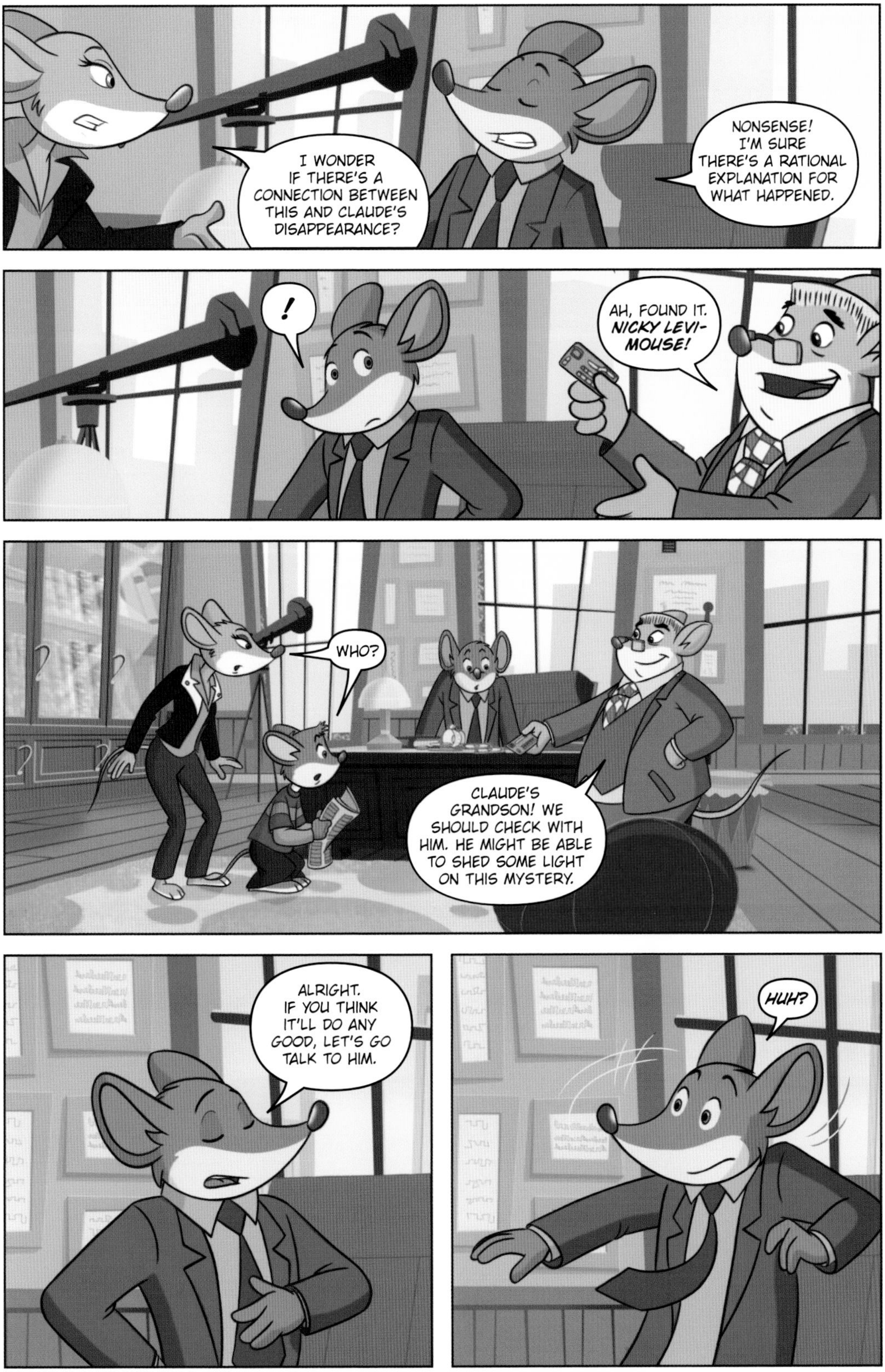
I WONDER IF THERE'S A CONNECTION BETWEEN THIS AND CLAUDE'S DISAPPEARANCE?
NONSENSE! I'M SURE THERE'S A RATIONAL EXPLANATION FOR WHAT HAPPENED.
!
AH, FOUND IT. NICKY LEVI-MOUSE!
WHO?
CLAUDE'S GRANDSON! WE SHOULD CHECK WITH HIM. HE MIGHT BE ABLE TO SHED SOME LIGHT ON THIS MYSTERY.
ALRIGHT. IF YOU THINK IT'LL DO ANY GOOD, LET'S GO TALK TO HIM.
HUH?

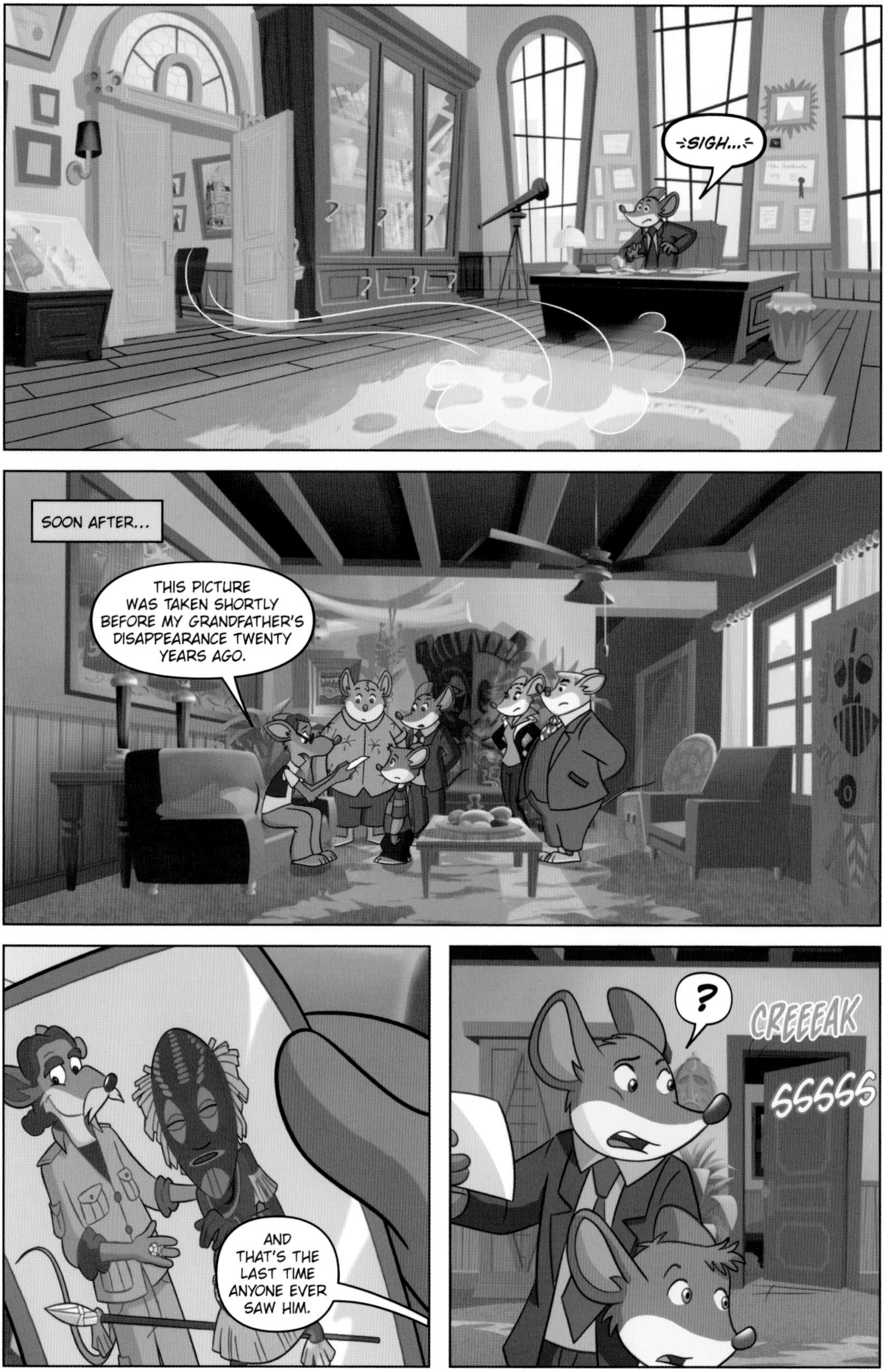
SIGH...
SOON AFTER...
THIS PICTURE WAS TAKEN SHORTLY BEFORE MY GRANDFATHER'S DISAPPEARANCE TWENTY YEARS AGO.
AND THAT'S THE LAST TIME ANYONE EVER SAW HIM.
?
CREEEAK
SSSSS

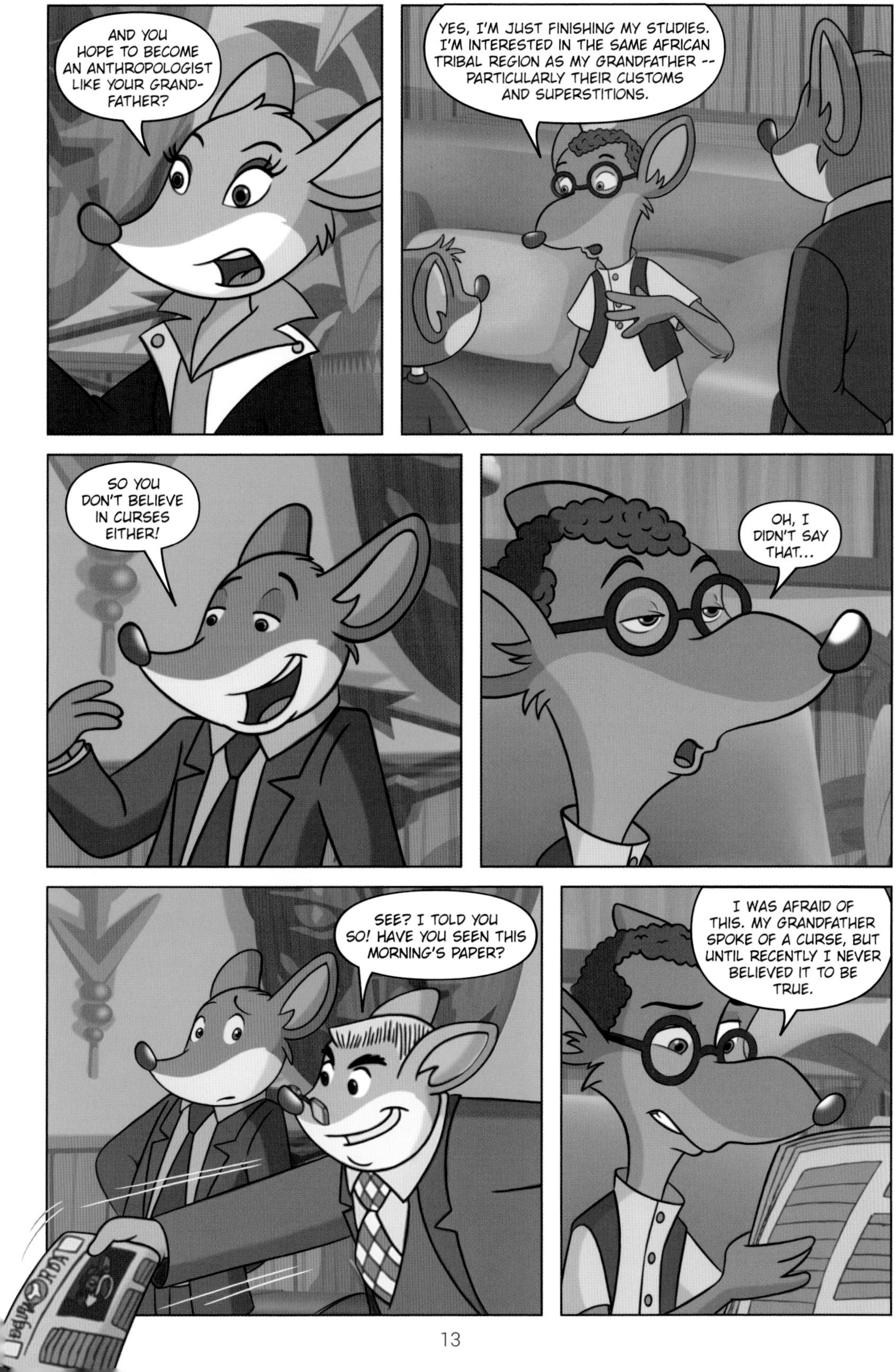
AND YOU HOPE TO BECOME AN ANTHROPOLOGIST LIKE YOUR GRAND-FATHER?
YES, I'M JUST FINISHING MY STUDIES. I'M INTERESTED IN THE SAME AFRICAN TRIBAL REGION AS MY GRANDFATHER -- PARTICULARLY THEIR CUSTOMS AND SUPERSTITIONS.
SO YOU DON'T BELIEVE IN CURSES EITHER!
OH, I DIDN'T SAY THAT...
SEE? I TOLD YOU SO! HAVE YOU SEEN THIS MORNING'S PAPER?
I WAS AFRAID OF THIS. MY GRANDFATHER SPOKE OF A CURSE, BUT UNTIL RECENTLY I NEVER BELIEVED IT TO BE TRUE.

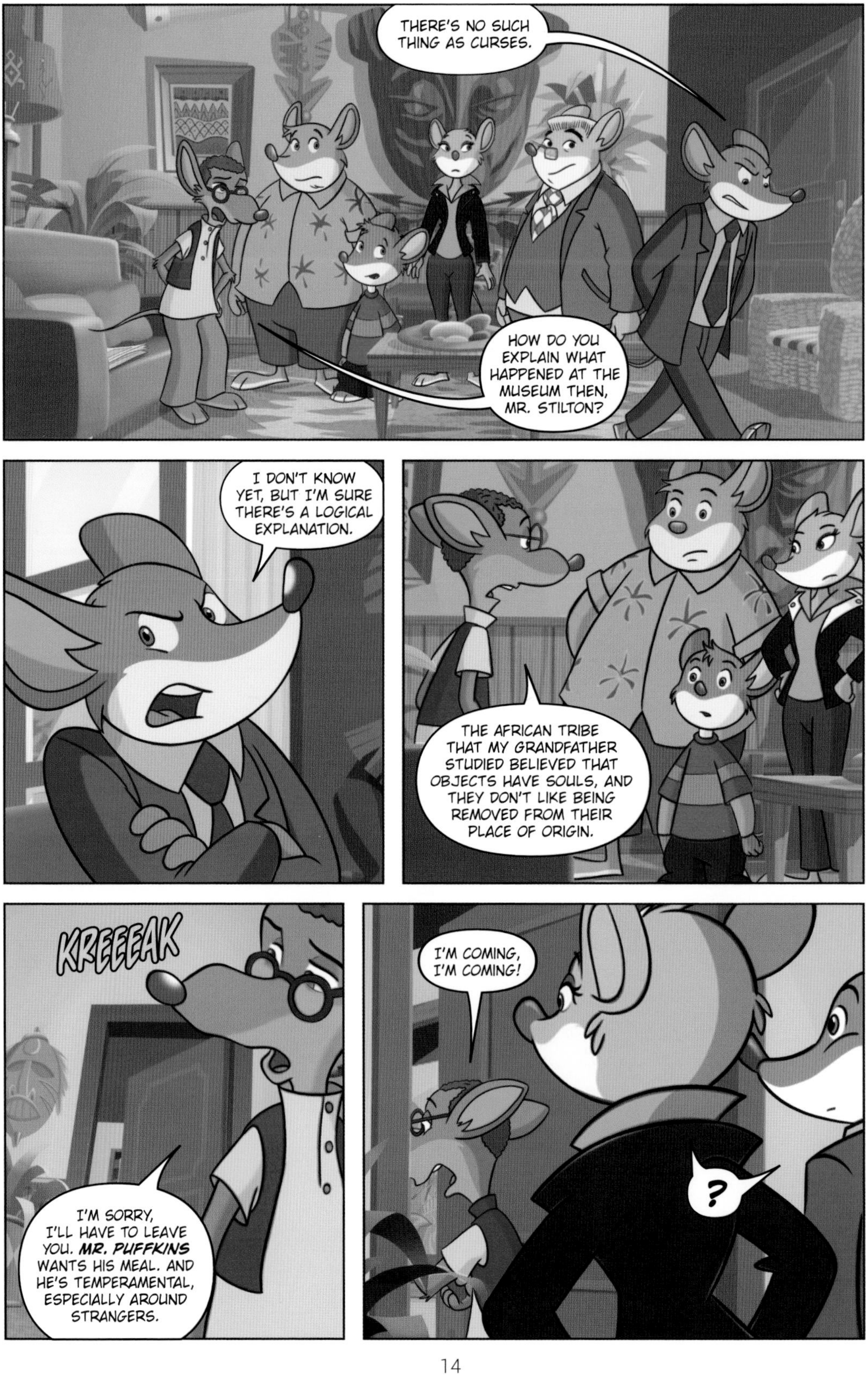
THERE'S NO SUCH THING AS CURSES.
HOW DO YOU EXPLAIN WHAT HAPPENED AT THE MUSEUM THEN, MR. STILTON?
I DON'T KNOW YET, BUT I'M SURE THERE'S A LOGICAL EXPLANATION.
THE AFRICAN TRIBE THAT MY GRANDFATHER STUDIED BELIEVED THAT OBJECTS HAVE SOULS, AND THEY DON'T LIKE BEING REMOVED FROM THEIR PLACE OF ORIGIN.
KREEEAK
I'M SORRY, I'LL HAVE TO LEAVE YOU. **MR. PUFFKINS** WANTS HIS MEAL. AND HE'S TEMPERAMENTAL, ESPECIALLY AROUND STRANGERS.
I'M COMING, I'M COMING!
?

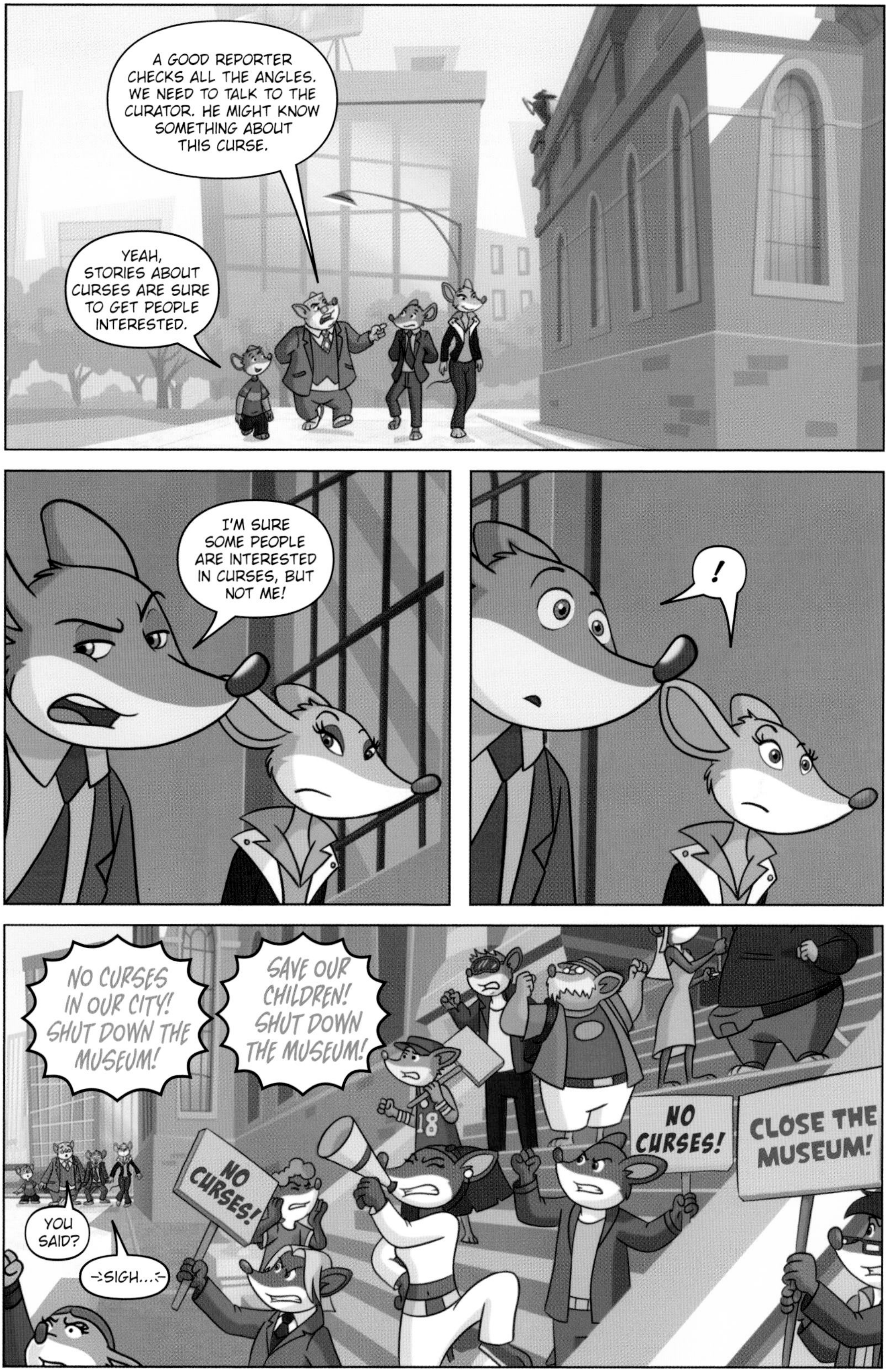
A GOOD REPORTER CHECKS ALL THE ANGLES. WE NEED TO TALK TO THE CURATOR. HE MIGHT KNOW SOMETHING ABOUT THIS CURSE.
YEAH, STORIES ABOUT CURSES ARE SURE TO GET PEOPLE INTERESTED.
I'M SURE SOME PEOPLE ARE INTERESTED IN CURSES, BUT NOT ME!
!
NO CURSES IN OUR CITY! SHUT DOWN THE MUSEUM!
SAVE OUR CHILDREN! SHUT DOWN THE MUSEUM!
NO CURSES!
CLOSE THE MUSEUM!
NO CURSES!
18
YOU SAID?
-SIGH...-

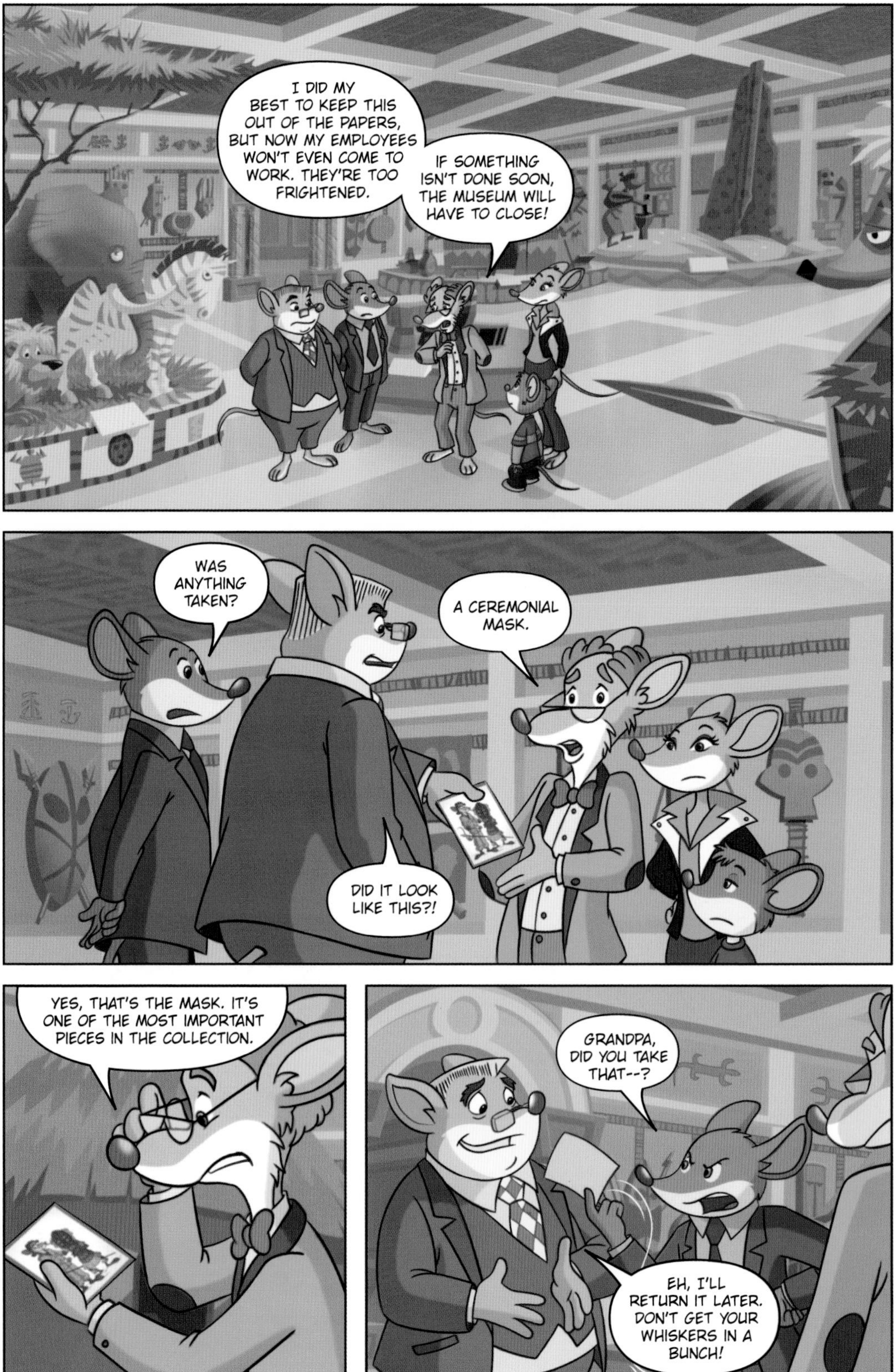
I DID MY BEST TO KEEP THIS OUT OF THE PAPERS, BUT NOW MY EMPLOYEES WON'T EVEN COME TO WORK. THEY'RE TOO FRIGHTENED.
IF SOMETHING ISN'T DONE SOON, THE MUSEUM WILL HAVE TO CLOSE!
WAS ANYTHING TAKEN?
A CEREMONIAL MASK.
DID IT LOOK LIKE THIS?!
YES, THAT'S THE MASK. IT'S ONE OF THE MOST IMPORTANT PIECES IN THE COLLECTION.
GRANDPA, DID YOU TAKE THAT--?
EH, I'LL RETURN IT LATER. DON'T GET YOUR WHISKERS IN A BUNCH!

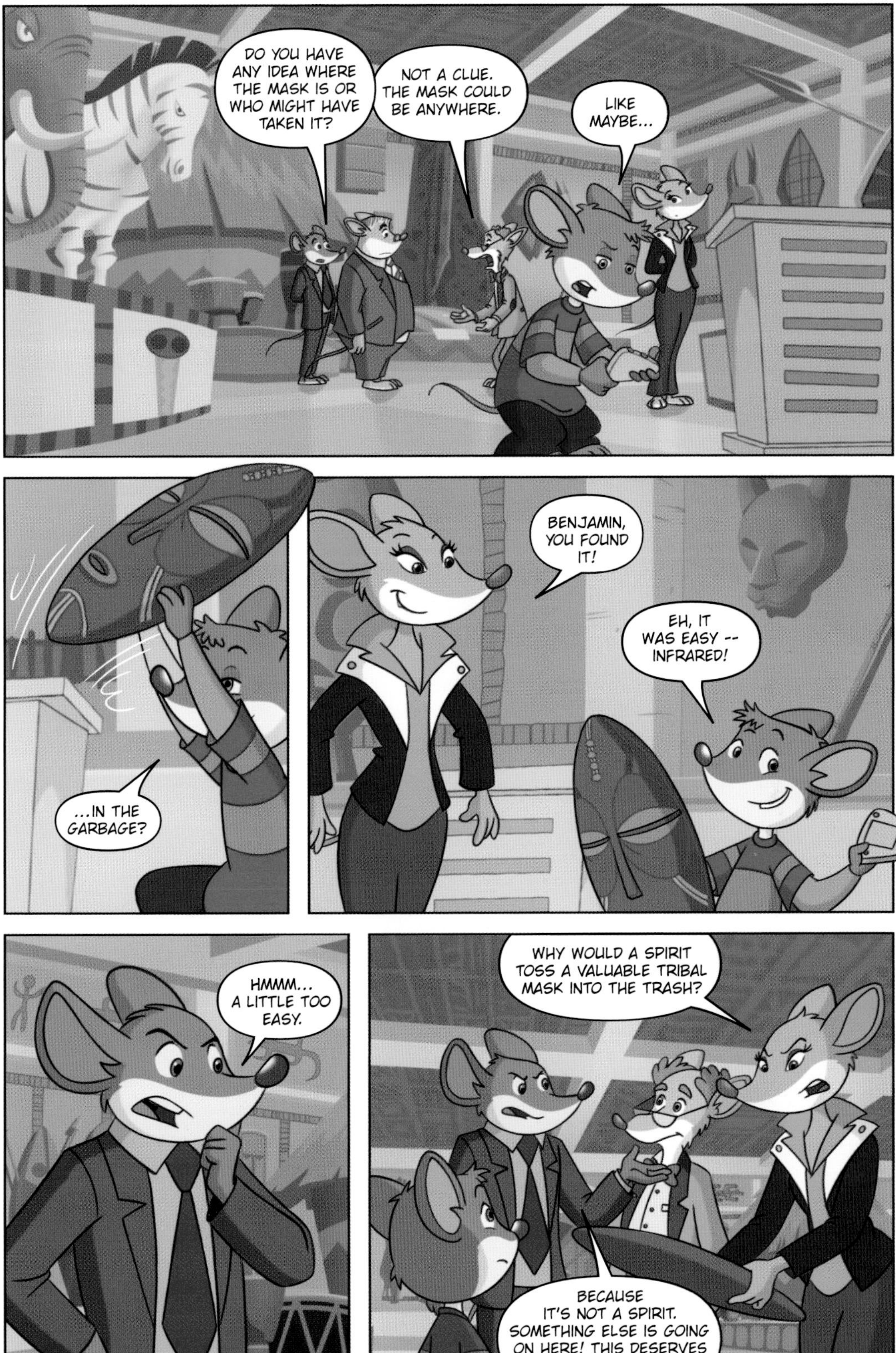
DO YOU HAVE ANY IDEA WHERE THE MASK IS OR WHO MIGHT HAVE TAKEN IT?
NOT A CLUE. THE MASK COULD BE ANYWHERE.
LIKE MAYBE...
...IN THE GARBAGE?
BENJAMIN, YOU FOUND IT!
EH, IT WAS EASY -- INFRARED!
HMMM... A LITTLE TOO EASY.
WHY WOULD A SPIRIT TOSS A VALUABLE TRIBAL MASK INTO THE TRASH?
BECAUSE IT'S NOT A SPIRIT. SOMETHING ELSE IS GOING ON HERE! THIS DESERVES A CLOSER LOOK.

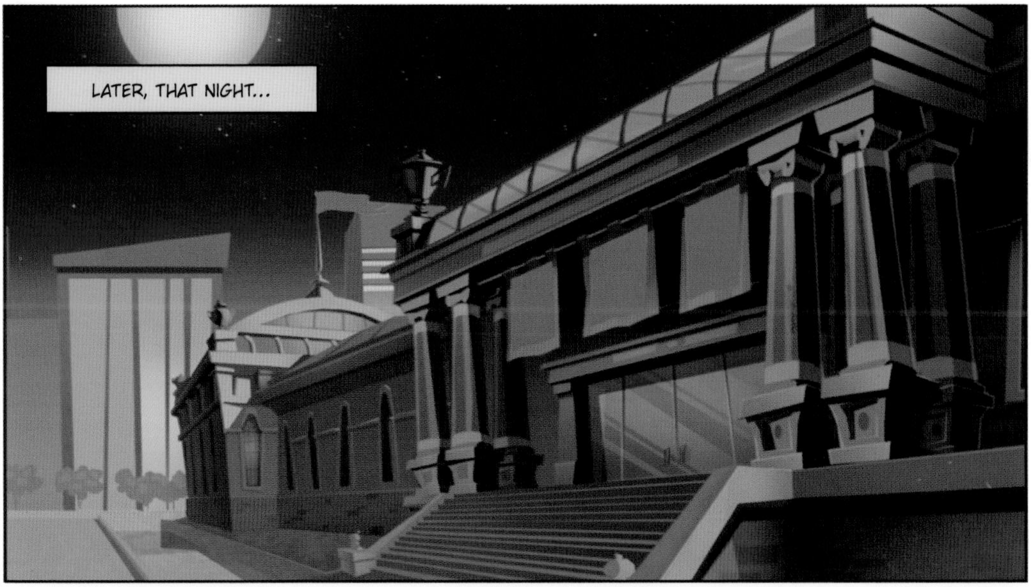
LATER, THAT NIGHT...

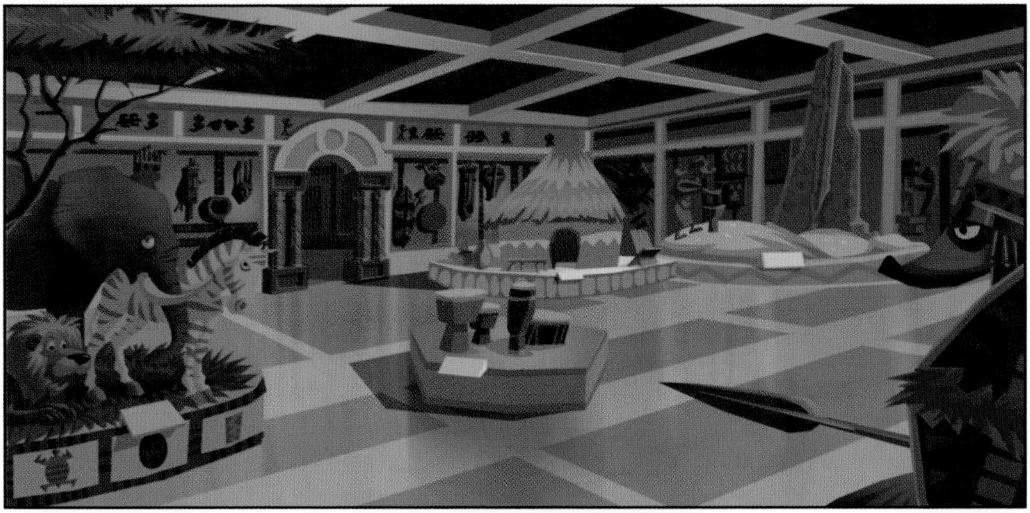

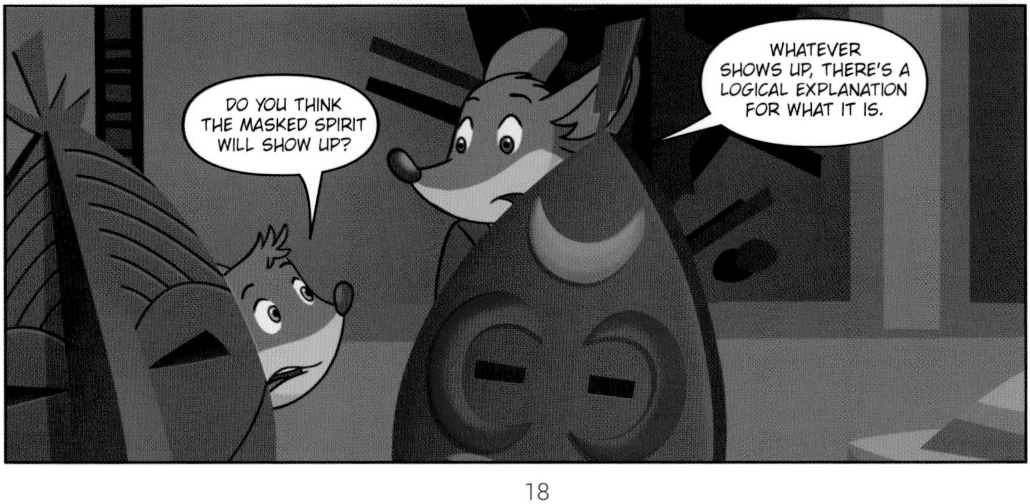
DO YOU THINK THE MASKED SPIRIT WILL SHOW UP?
WHATEVER SHOWS UP, THERE'S A LOGICAL EXPLANATION FOR WHAT IT IS.

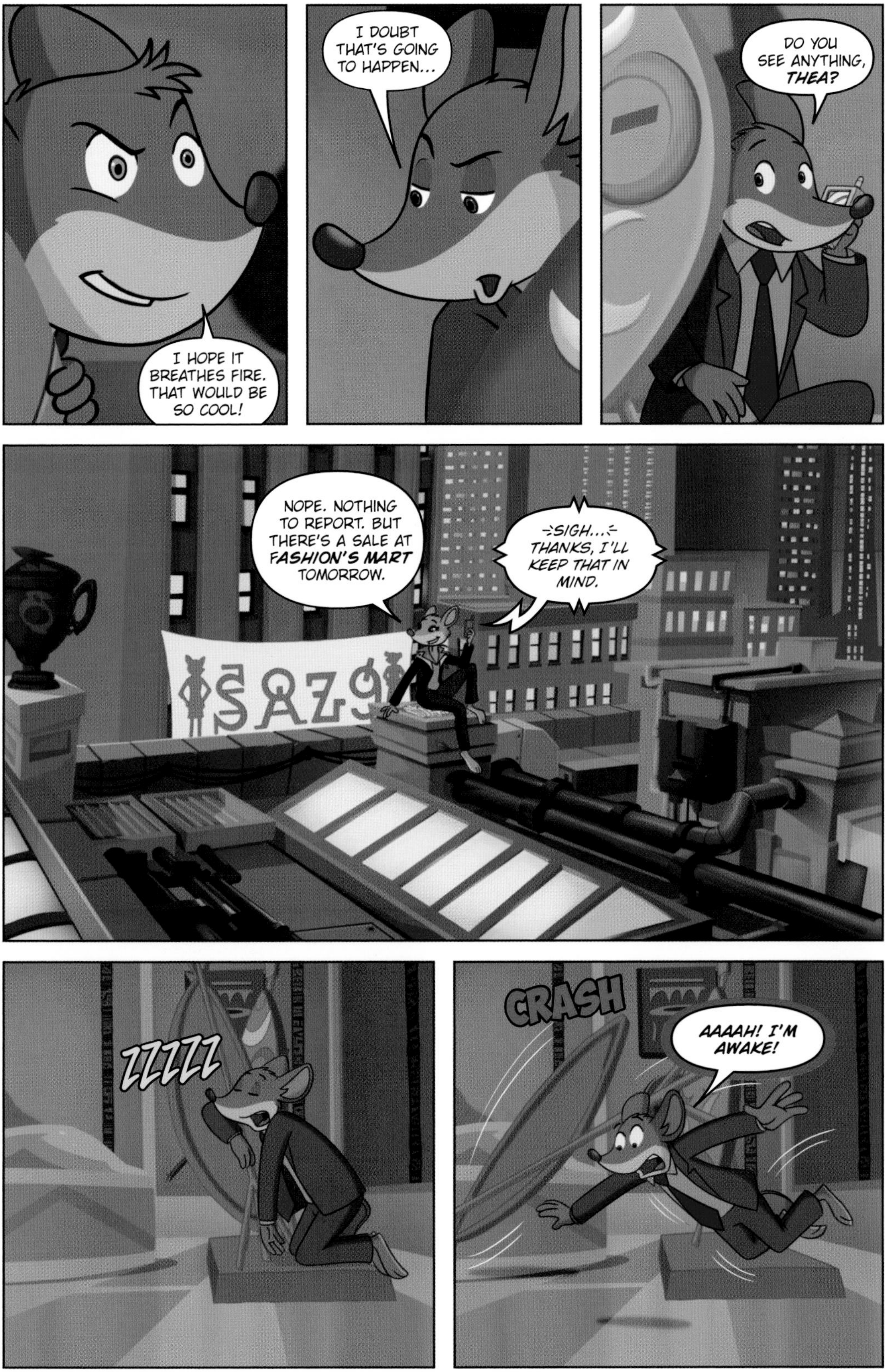
I HOPE IT BREATHES FIRE. THAT WOULD BE SO COOL!
I DOUBT THAT'S GOING TO HAPPEN...
DO YOU SEE ANYTHING, *THEA?*
NOPE. NOTHING TO REPORT. BUT THERE'S A SALE AT ***FASHION'S MART*** TOMORROW.
SIGH... THANKS, I'LL KEEP THAT IN MIND.
ZZZZZ
CRASH
AAAAH! I'M AWAKE!

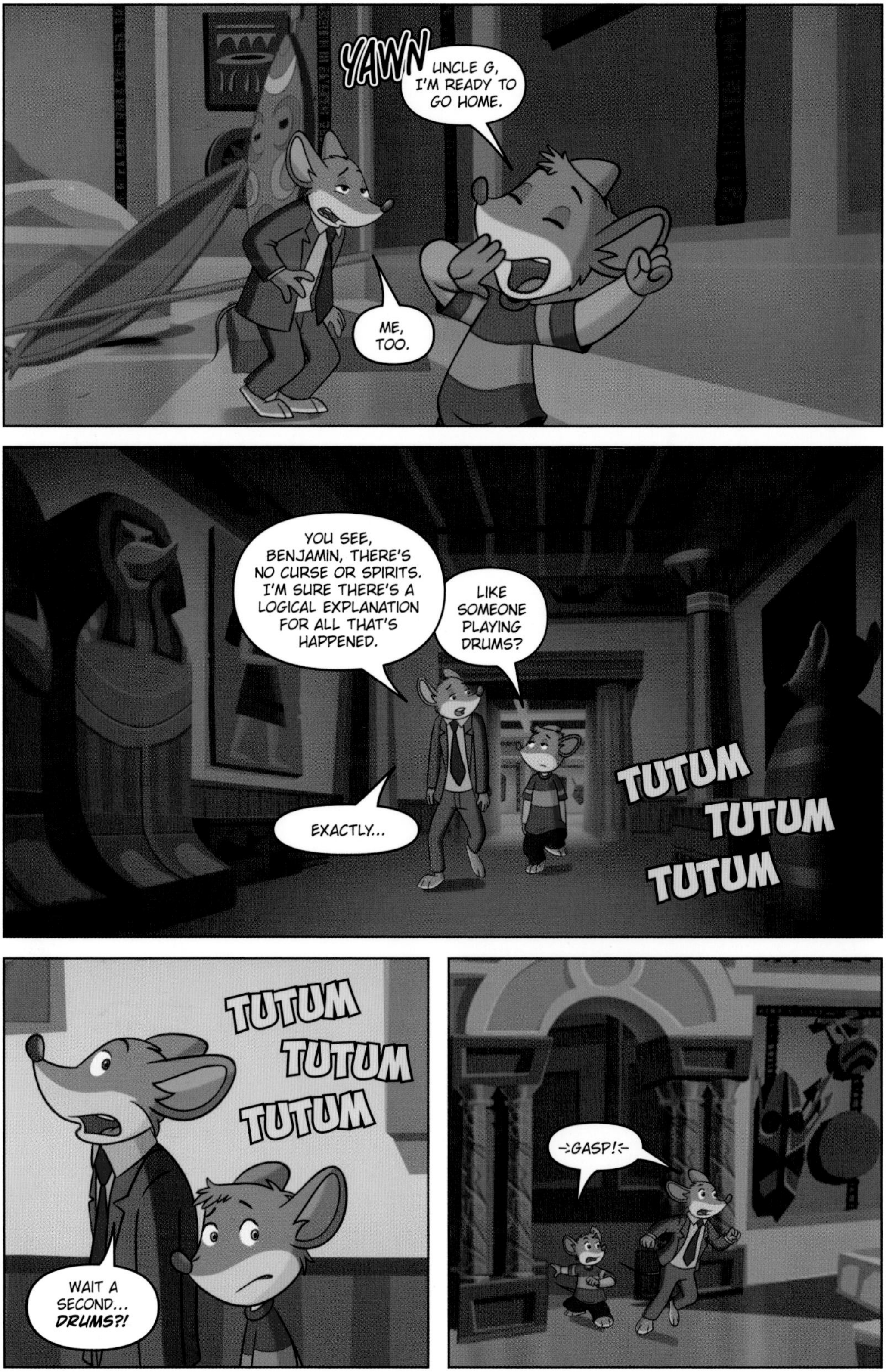
YAWN
UNCLE G, I'M READY TO GO HOME.
ME, TOO.
YOU SEE, BENJAMIN, THERE'S NO CURSE OR SPIRITS. I'M SURE THERE'S A LOGICAL EXPLANATION FOR ALL THAT'S HAPPENED.
LIKE SOMEONE PLAYING DRUMS?
EXACTLY...
TUTUM TUTUM TUTUM
TUTUM TUTUM TUTUM
WAIT A SECOND... ***DRUMS?!***
-GASP!-

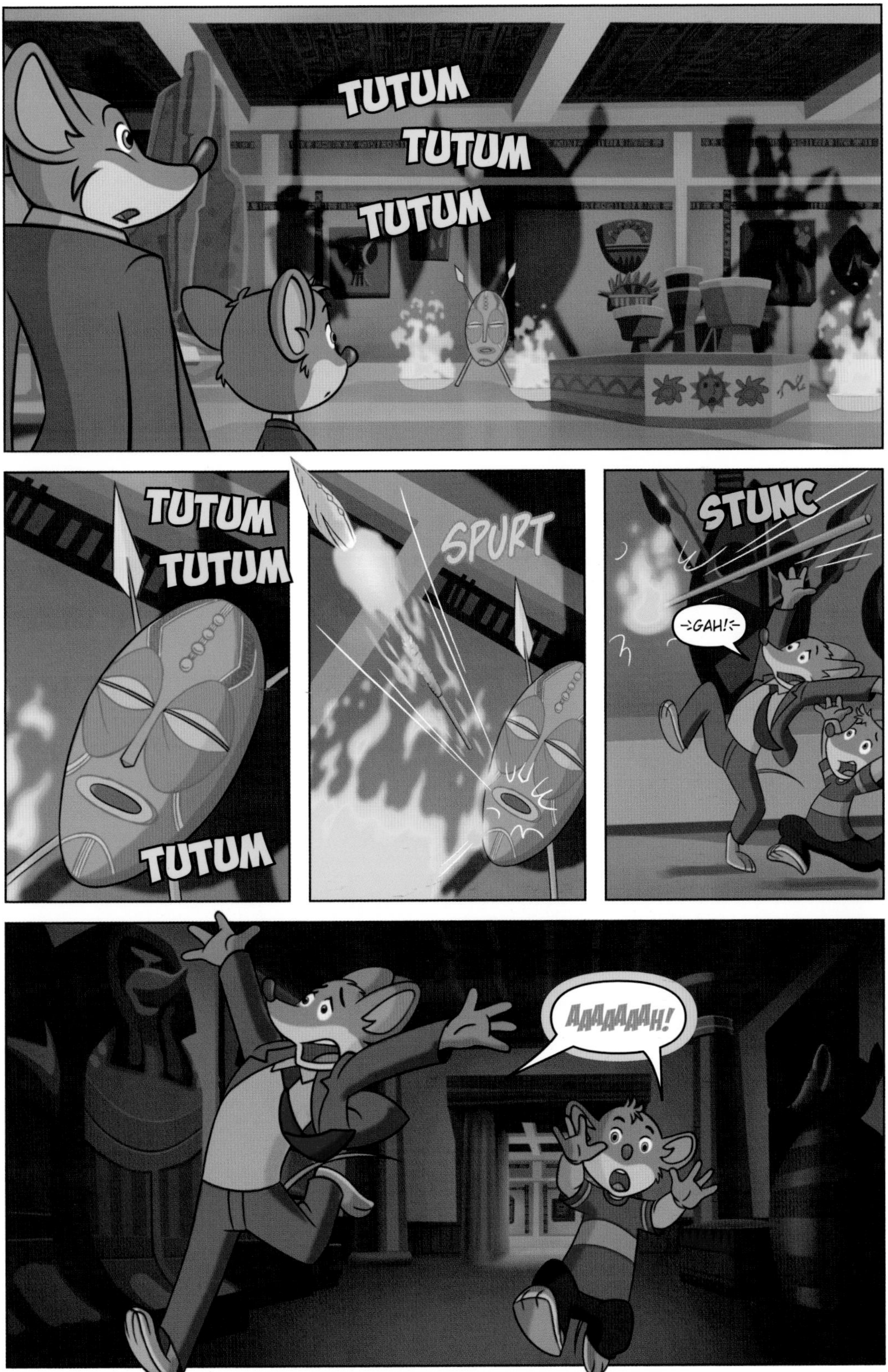
TUTUM
TUTUM
TUTUM
TUTUM
TUTUM
TUTUM
SPURT
STUNC
GAH!
AAAAAAAH!

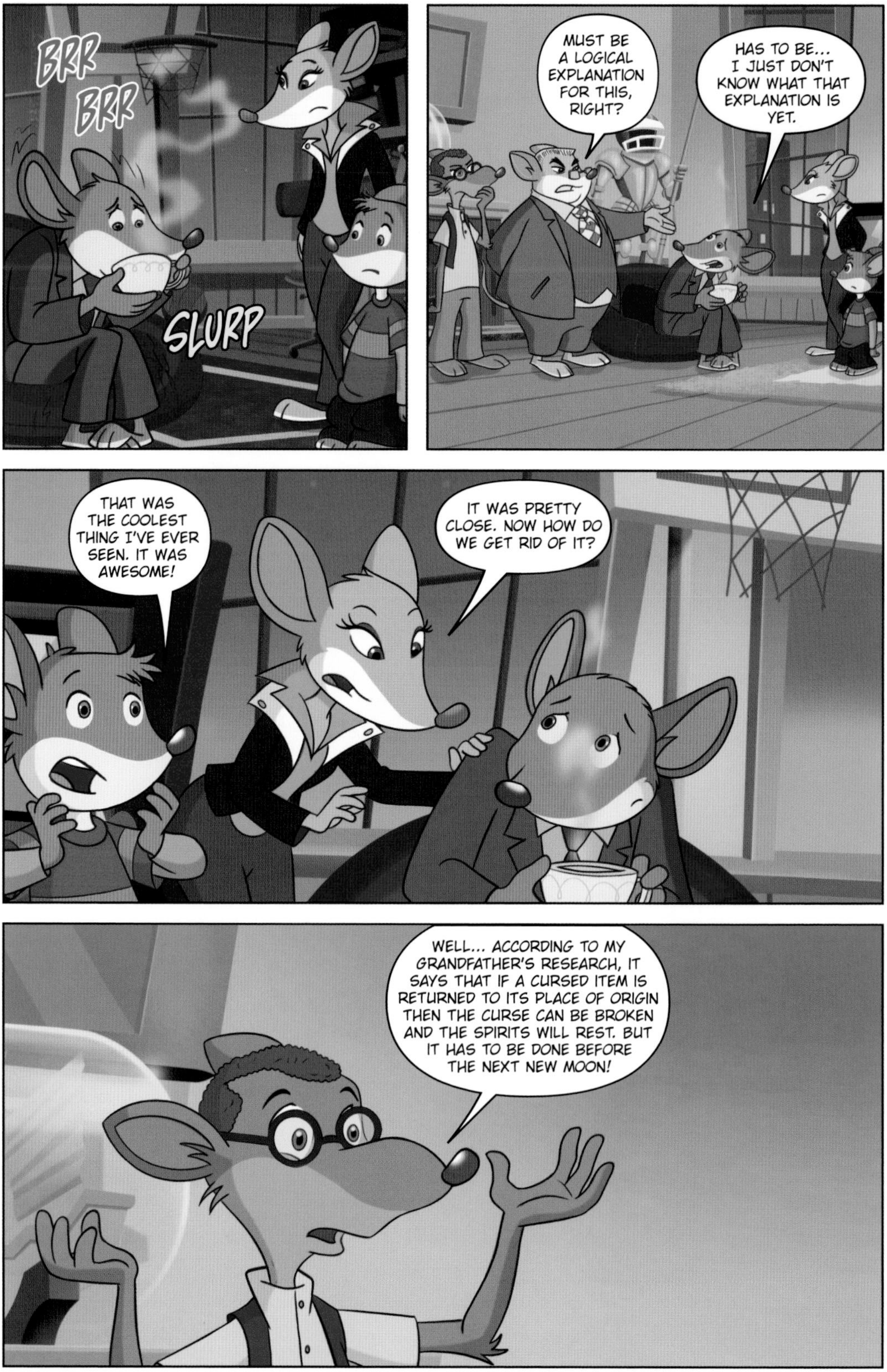
BRR
BRR
SLURP
MUST BE A LOGICAL EXPLANATION FOR THIS, RIGHT?
HAS TO BE... I JUST DON'T KNOW WHAT THAT EXPLANATION IS YET.
THAT WAS THE COOLEST THING I'VE EVER SEEN. IT WAS AWESOME!
IT WAS PRETTY CLOSE. NOW HOW DO WE GET RID OF IT?
WELL... ACCORDING TO MY GRANDFATHER'S RESEARCH, IT SAYS THAT IF A CURSED ITEM IS RETURNED TO ITS PLACE OF ORIGIN THEN THE CURSE CAN BE BROKEN AND THE SPIRITS WILL REST. BUT IT HAS TO BE DONE BEFORE THE NEXT NEW MOON!

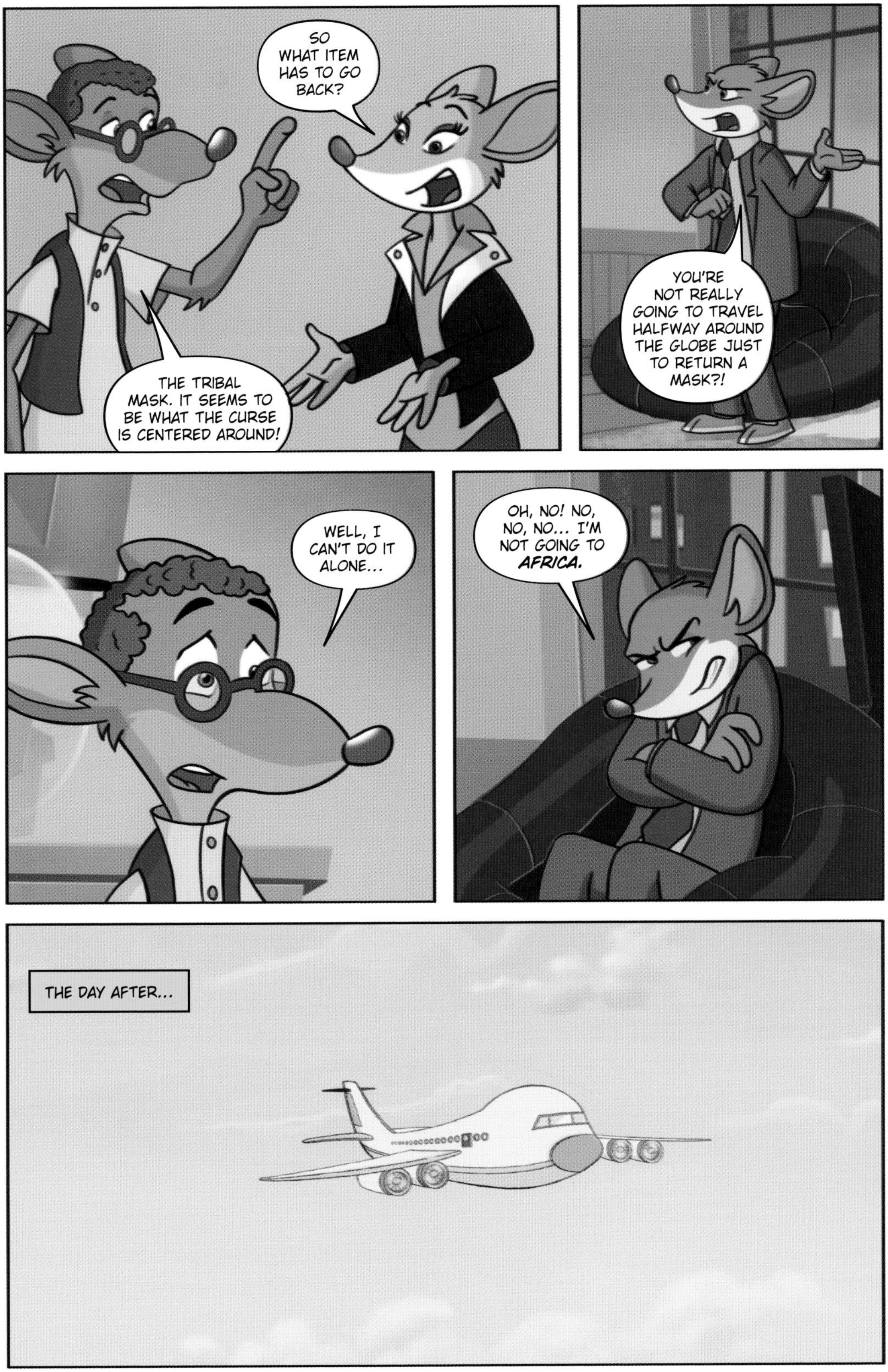
SO WHAT ITEM HAS TO GO BACK?
THE TRIBAL MASK. IT SEEMS TO BE WHAT THE CURSE IS CENTERED AROUND!
YOU'RE NOT REALLY GOING TO TRAVEL HALFWAY AROUND THE GLOBE JUST TO RETURN A MASK?!
WELL, I CAN'T DO IT ALONE...
OH, NO! NO, NO, NO... I'M NOT GOING TO AFRICA.
THE DAY AFTER...

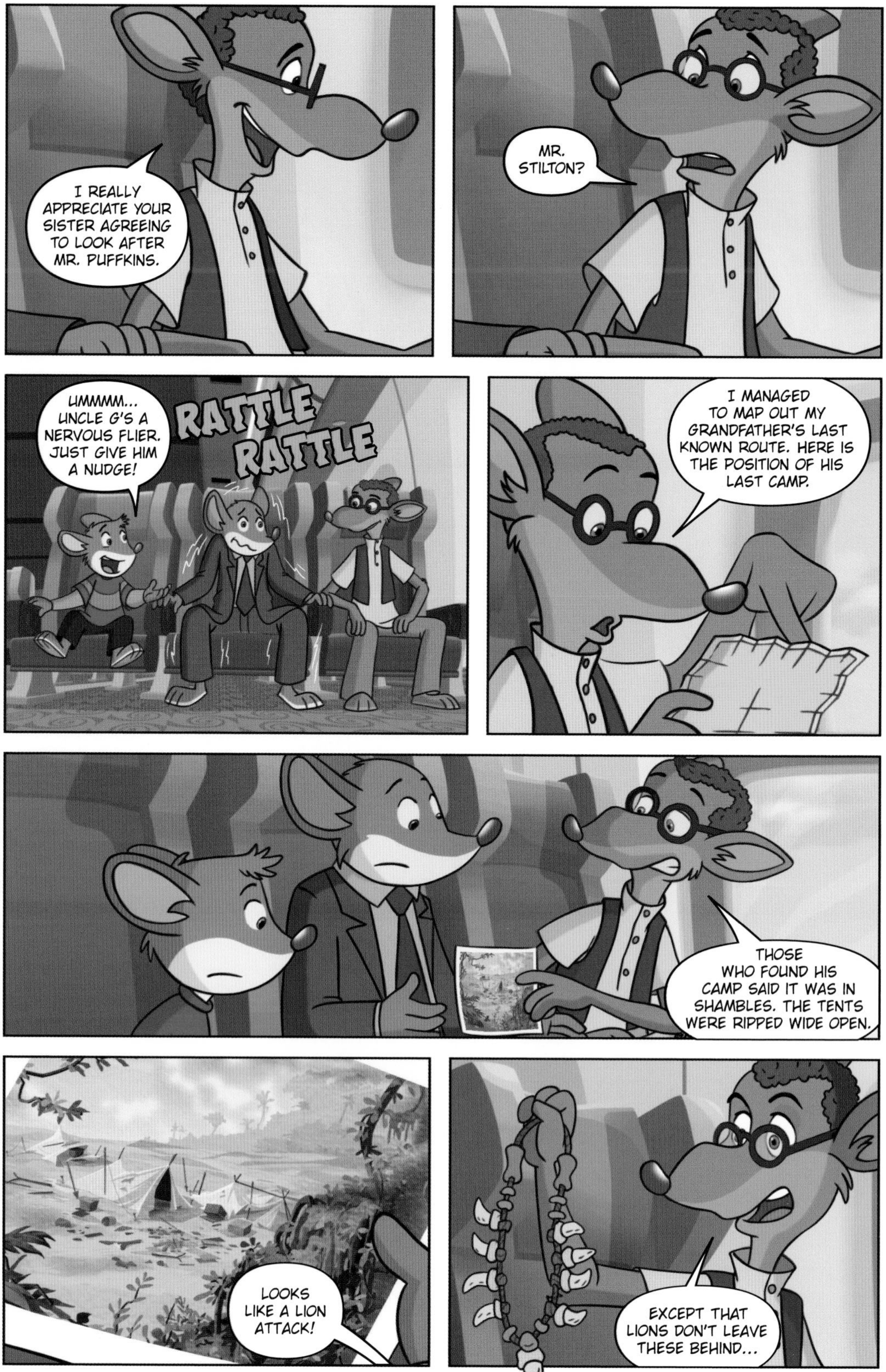
I REALLY APPRECIATE YOUR SISTER AGREEING TO LOOK AFTER MR. PUFFKINS.
MR. STILTON?
UMMMM... UNCLE G'S A NERVOUS FLIER. JUST GIVE HIM A NUDGE!
RATTLE RATTLE
I MANAGED TO MAP OUT MY GRANDFATHER'S LAST KNOWN ROUTE. HERE IS THE POSITION OF HIS LAST CAMP.
THOSE WHO FOUND HIS CAMP SAID IT WAS IN SHAMBLES. THE TENTS WERE RIPPED WIDE OPEN.
LOOKS LIKE A LION ATTACK!
EXCEPT THAT LIONS DON'T LEAVE THESE BEHIND...

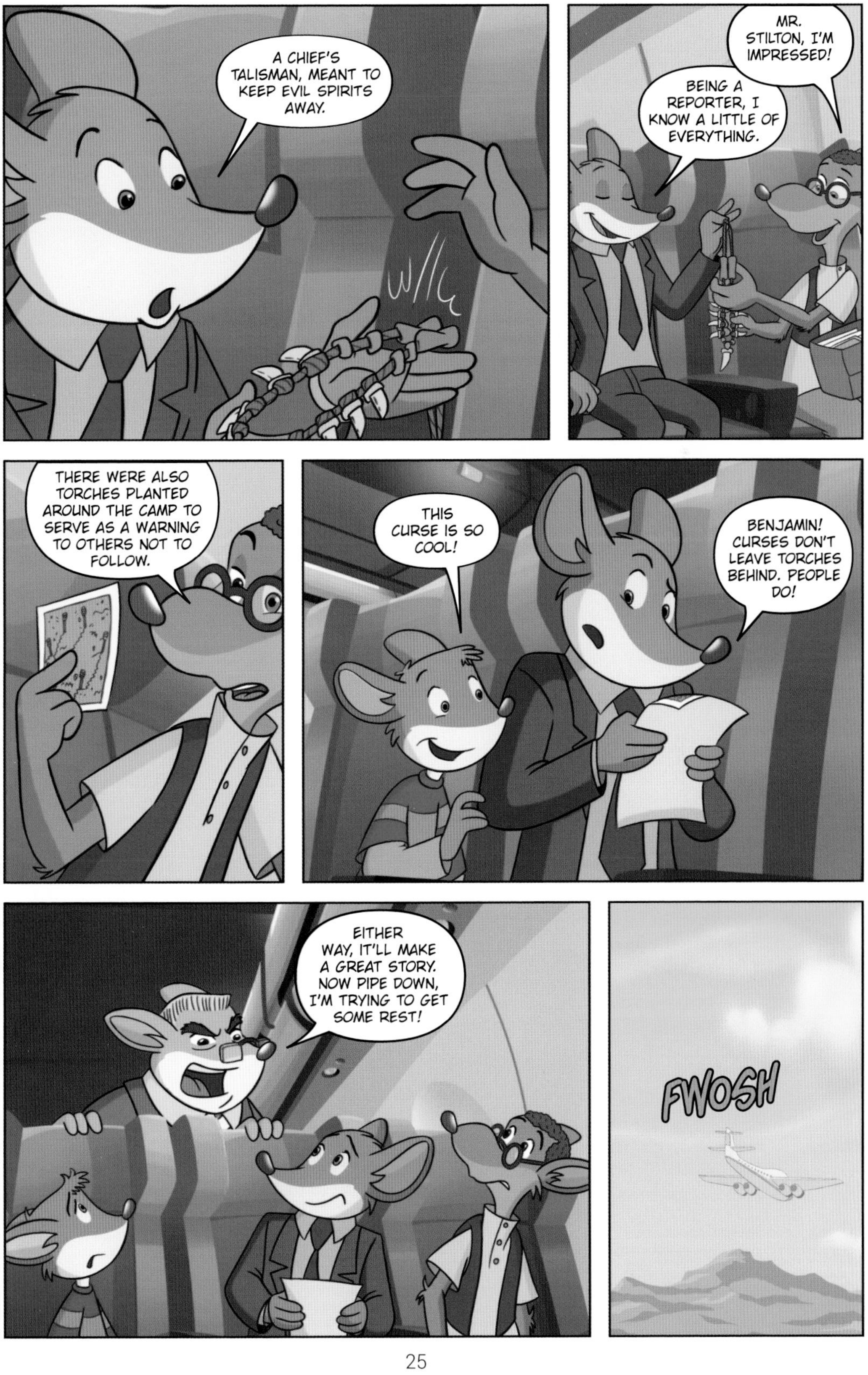
A CHIEF'S TALISMAN, MEANT TO KEEP EVIL SPIRITS AWAY.
MR. STILTON, I'M IMPRESSED!
BEING A REPORTER, I KNOW A LITTLE OF EVERYTHING.
THERE WERE ALSO TORCHES PLANTED AROUND THE CAMP TO SERVE AS A WARNING TO OTHERS NOT TO FOLLOW.
THIS CURSE IS SO COOL!
BENJAMIN! CURSES DON'T LEAVE TORCHES BEHIND. PEOPLE DO!
EITHER WAY, IT'LL MAKE A GREAT STORY. NOW PIPE DOWN, I'M TRYING TO GET SOME REST!
FWOSH

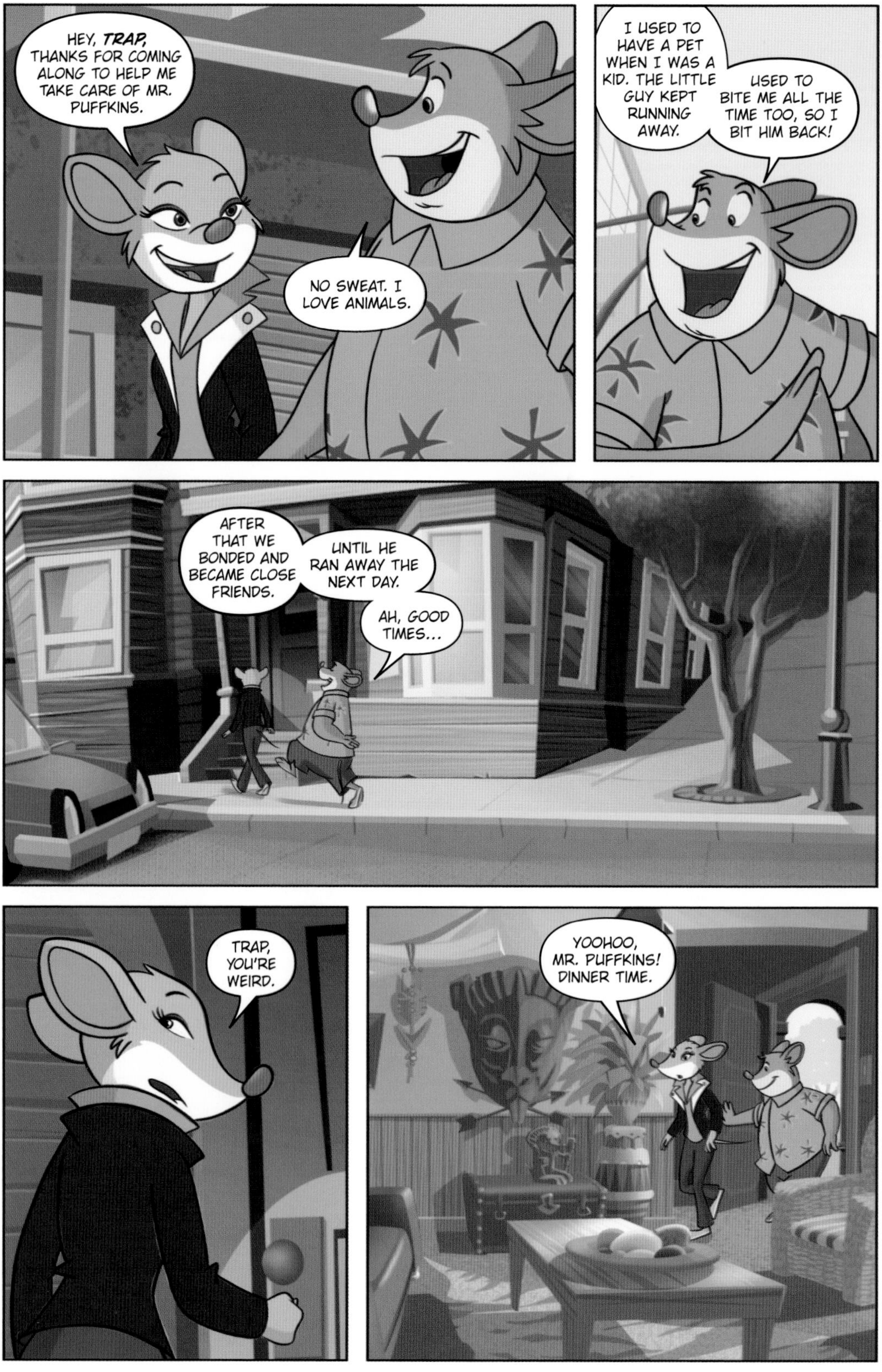
HEY, ***TRAP,*** THANKS FOR COMING ALONG TO HELP ME TAKE CARE OF MR. PUFFKINS.
NO SWEAT. I LOVE ANIMALS.
I USED TO HAVE A PET WHEN I WAS A KID. THE LITTLE GUY KEPT RUNNING AWAY.
USED TO BITE ME ALL THE TIME TOO, SO I BIT HIM BACK!
AFTER THAT WE BONDED AND BECAME CLOSE FRIENDS.
UNTIL HE RAN AWAY THE NEXT DAY.
AH, GOOD TIMES...
TRAP, YOU'RE WEIRD.
YOOHOO, MR. PUFFKINS! DINNER TIME.

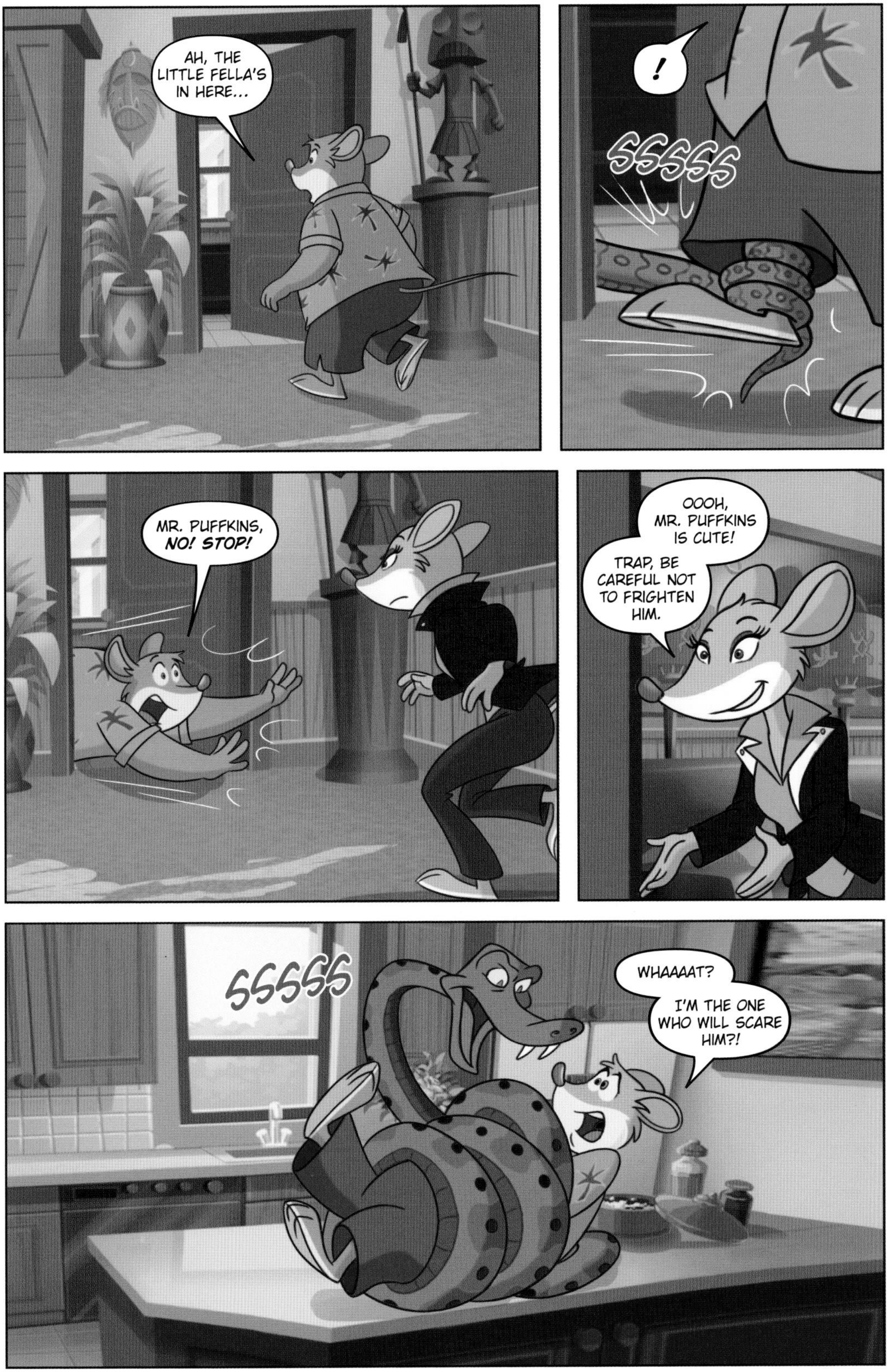
AH, THE LITTLE FELLA'S IN HERE...
!
SSSSS
MR. PUFFKINS, **NO! STOP!**
OOOH, MR. PUFFKINS IS CUTE!
TRAP, BE CAREFUL NOT TO FRIGHTEN HIM.
SSSSS
WHAAAAT?
I'M THE ONE WHO WILL SCARE HIM?!

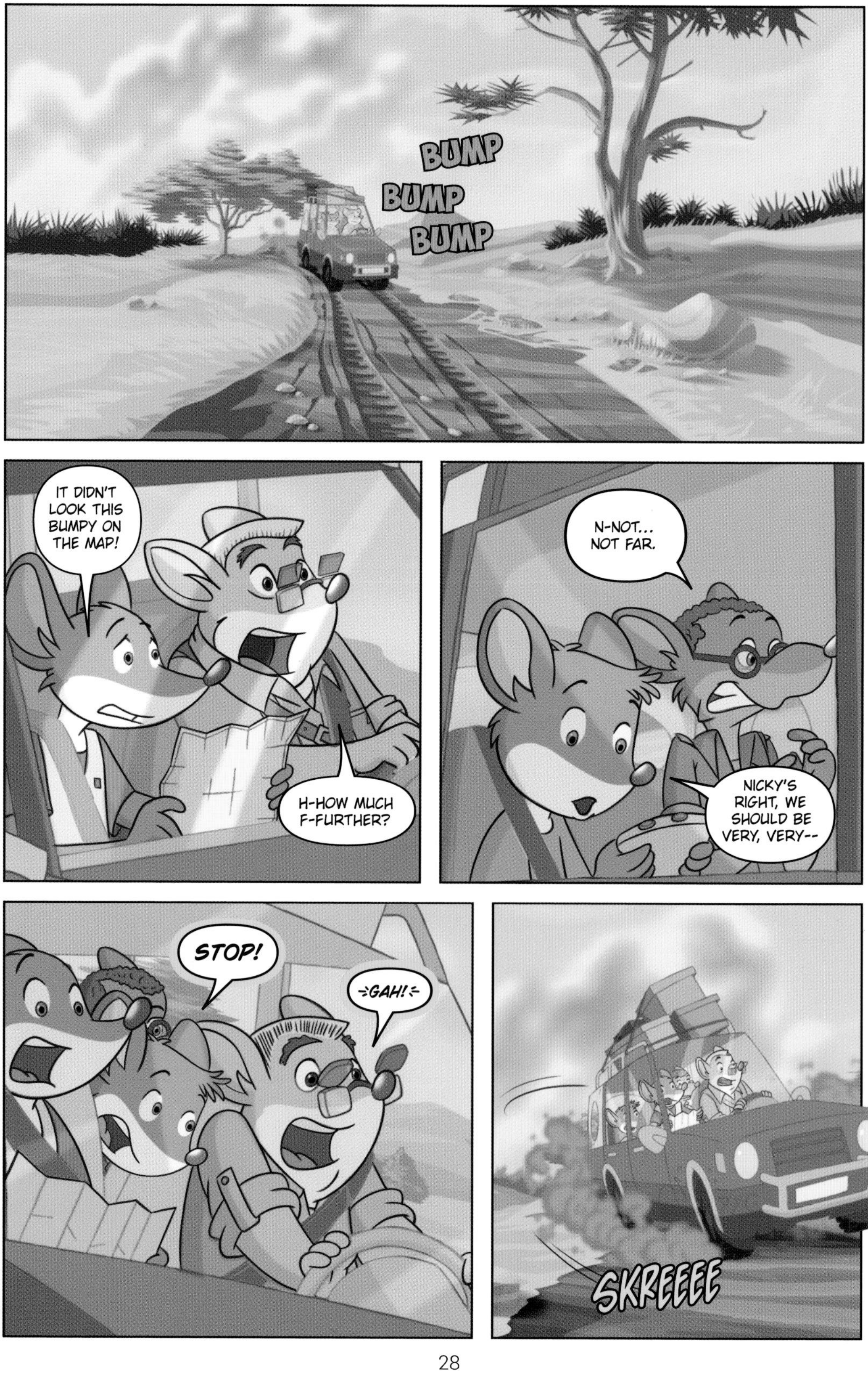
BUMP
BUMP
BUMP
IT DIDN'T LOOK THIS BUMPY ON THE MAP!
H-HOW MUCH F-FURTHER?
N-NOT... NOT FAR.
NICKY'S RIGHT, WE SHOULD BE VERY, VERY--
STOP!
GAH!
SKREEEE

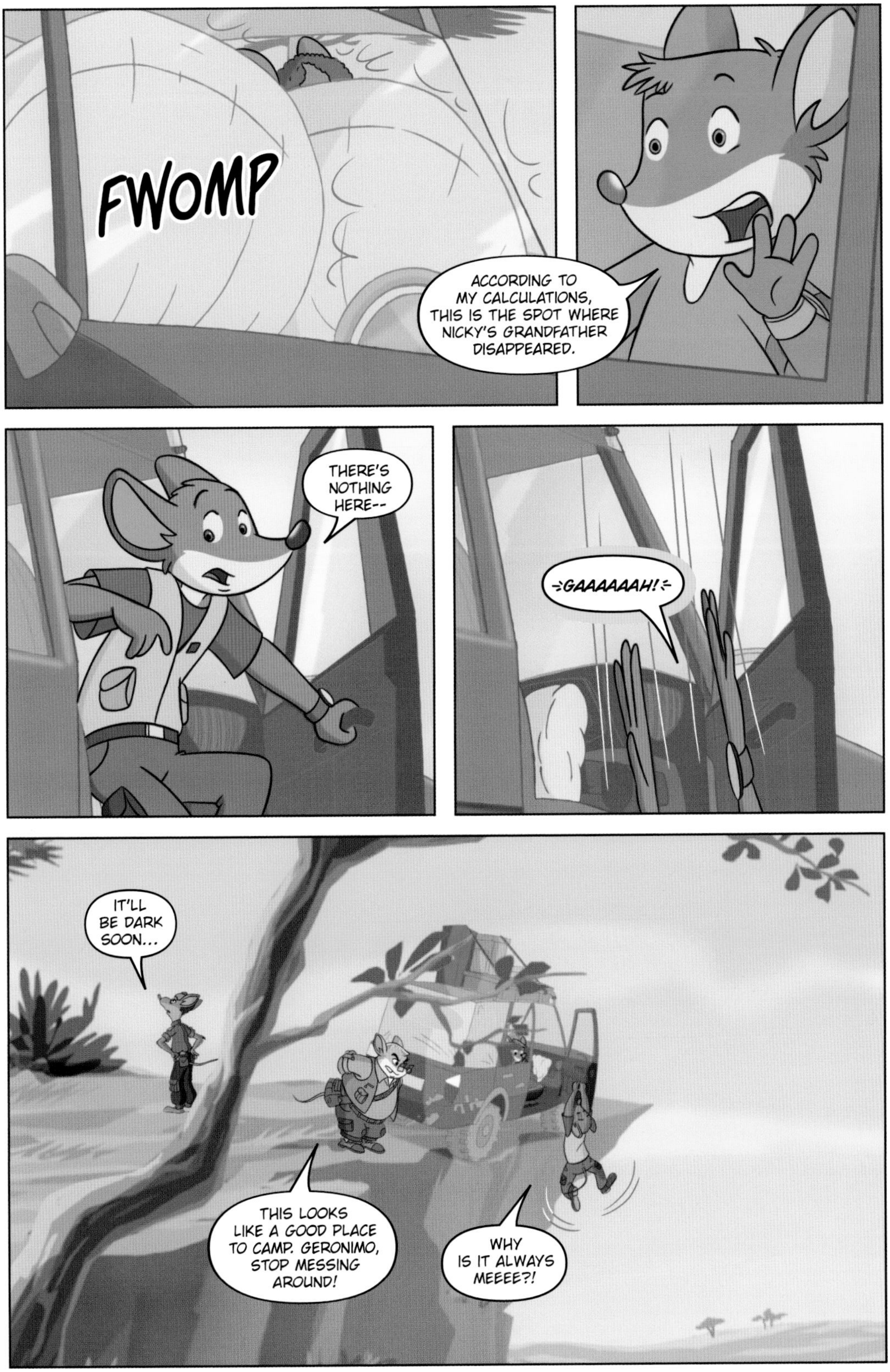
FWOMP
ACCORDING TO MY CALCULATIONS, THIS IS THE SPOT WHERE NICKY'S GRANDFATHER DISAPPEARED.
THERE'S NOTHING HERE--
GAAAAAAH!
IT'LL BE DARK SOON...
THIS LOOKS LIKE A GOOD PLACE TO CAMP. GERONIMO, STOP MESSING AROUND!
WHY IS IT ALWAYS MEEEE?!

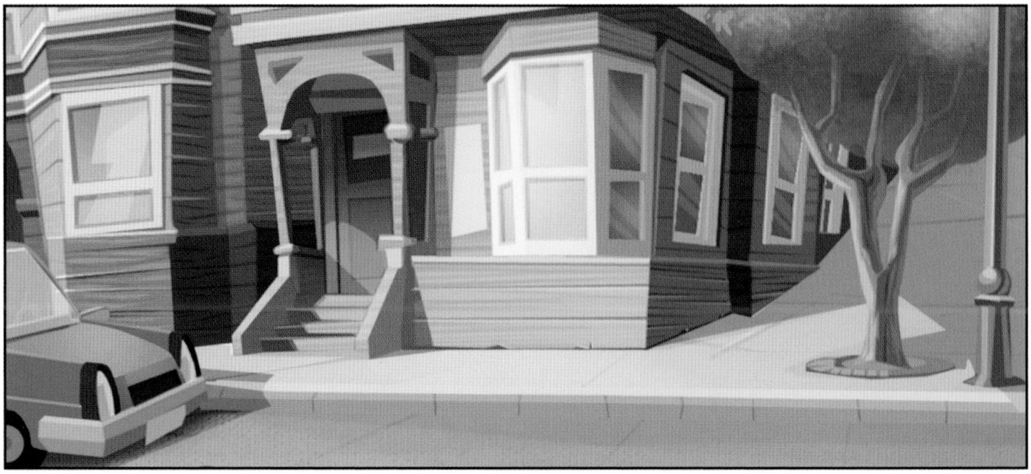

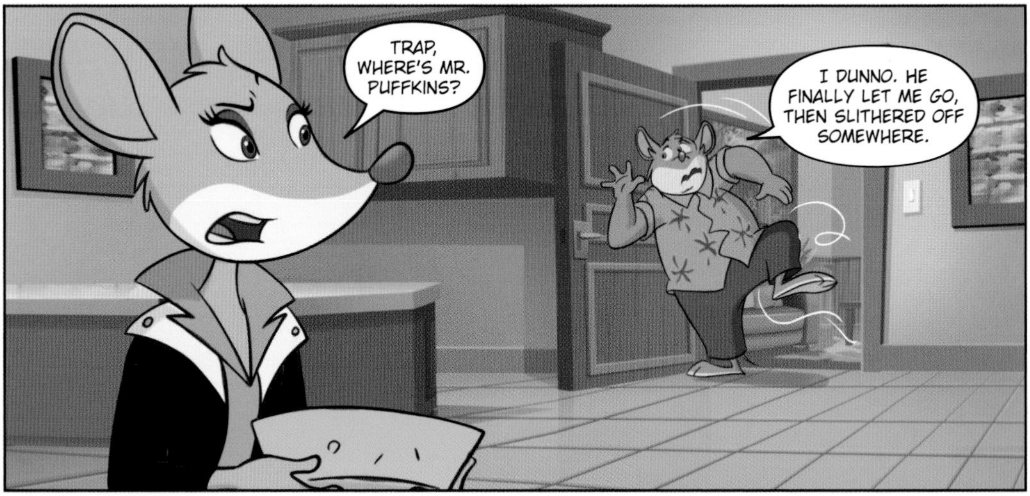
TRAP, WHERE'S MR. PUFFKINS?
I DUNNO. HE FINALLY LET ME GO, THEN SLITHERED OFF SOMEWHERE.

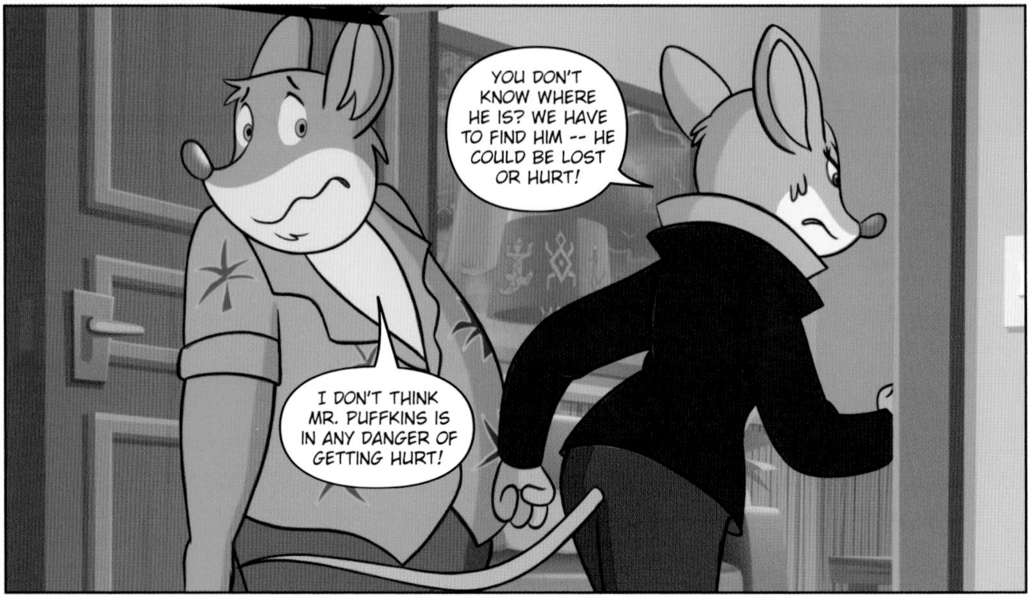
YOU DON'T KNOW WHERE HE IS? WE HAVE TO FIND HIM -- HE COULD BE LOST OR HURT!
I DON'T THINK MR. PUFFKINS IS IN ANY DANGER OF GETTING HURT!

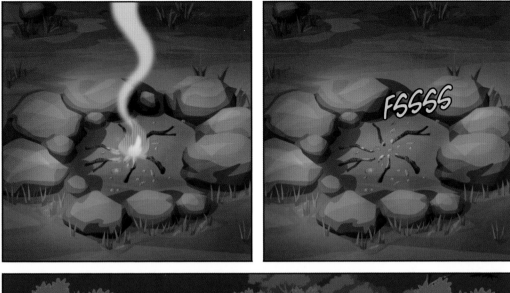

FSSSS

ZZZ   ZZZ   ZZZ   ZZZ

ZZZ

FWASH

HM?

⇥GASP!⇤

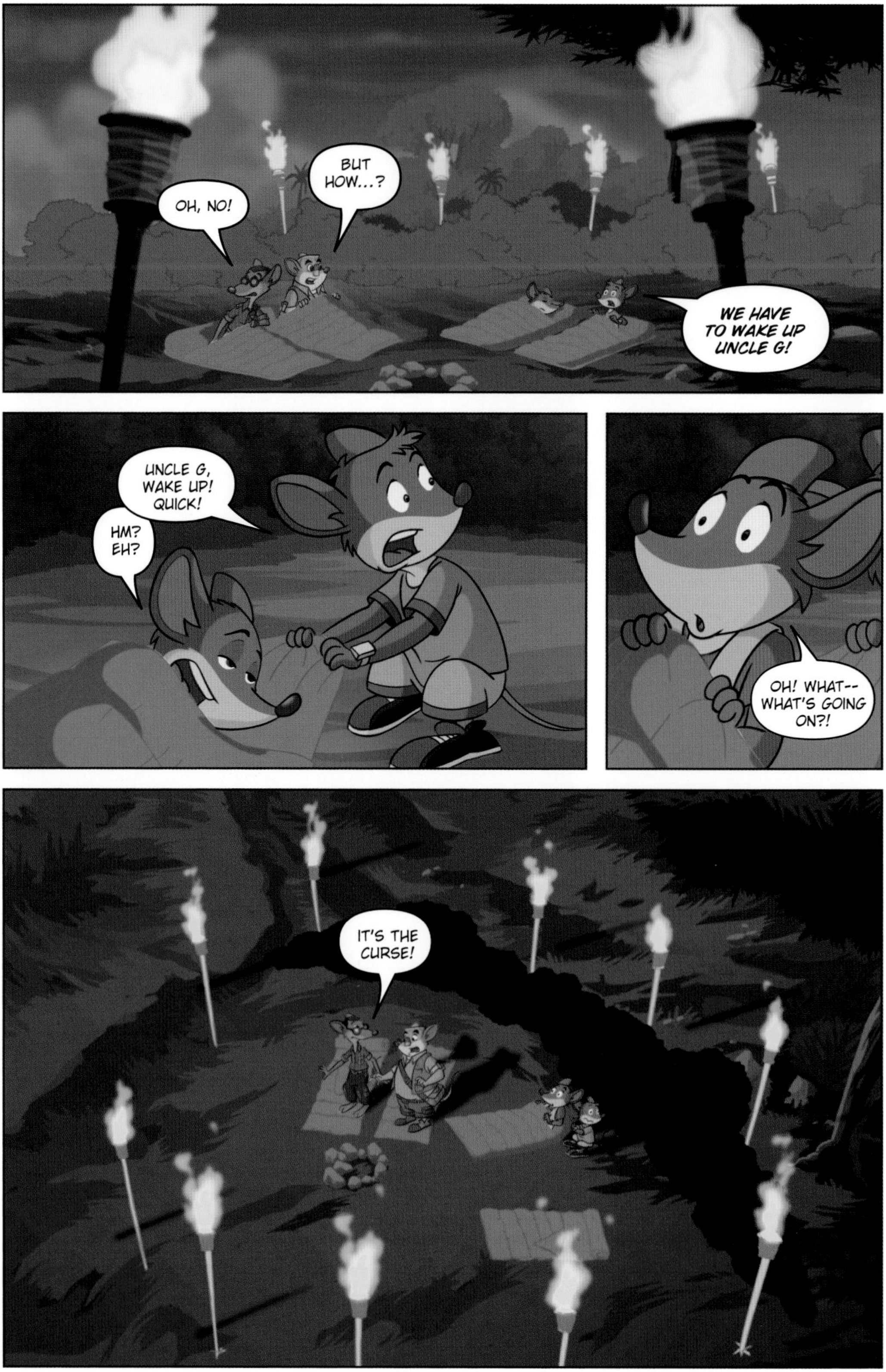
OH, NO!
BUT HOW...?
WE HAVE TO WAKE UP UNCLE G!
UNCLE G, WAKE UP! QUICK!
HM? EH?
OH! WHAT-- WHAT'S GOING ON?!
IT'S THE CURSE!

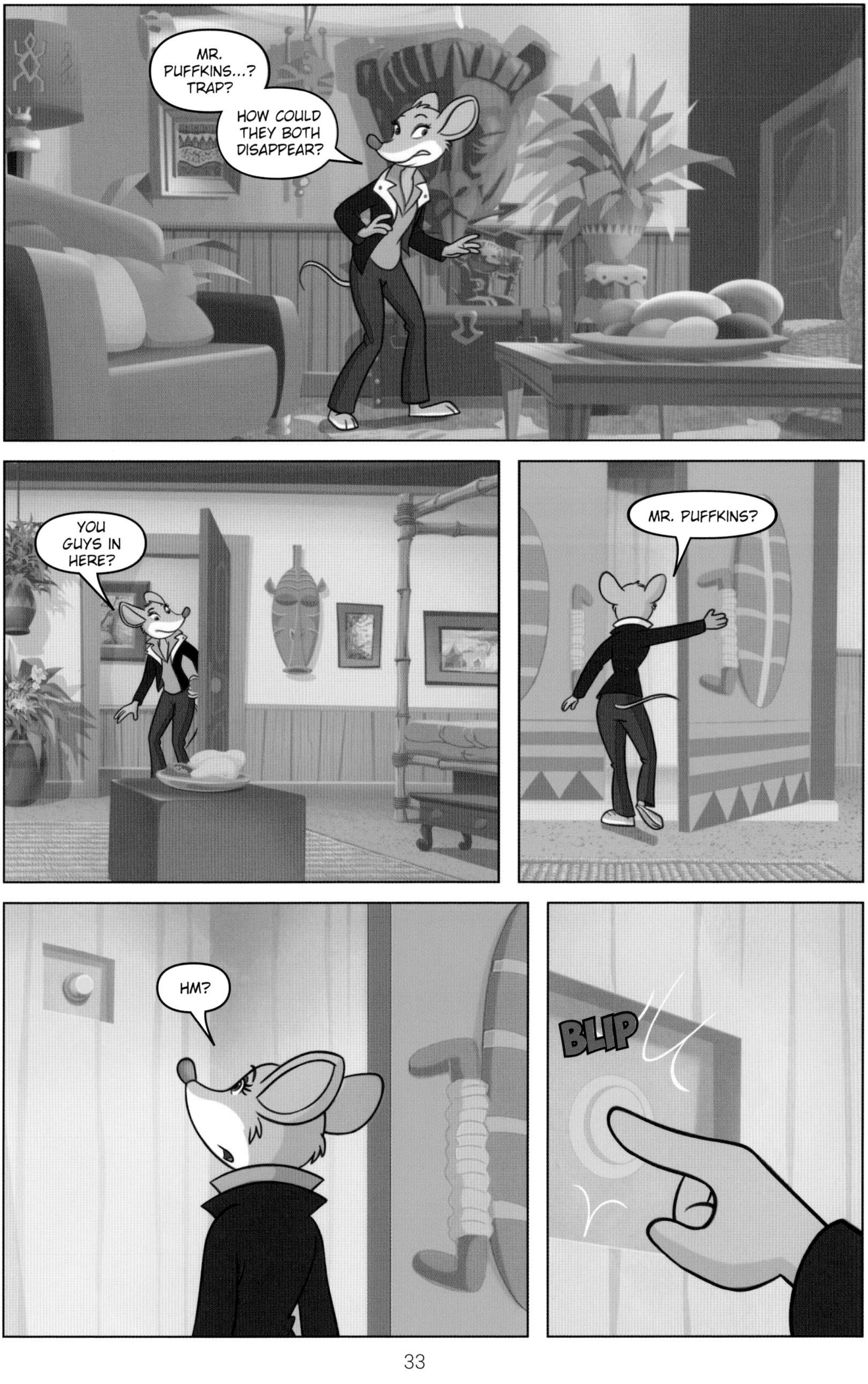
MR. PUFFKINS...? TRAP?
HOW COULD THEY BOTH DISAPPEAR?
YOU GUYS IN HERE?
MR. PUFFKINS?
HM?
BLIP

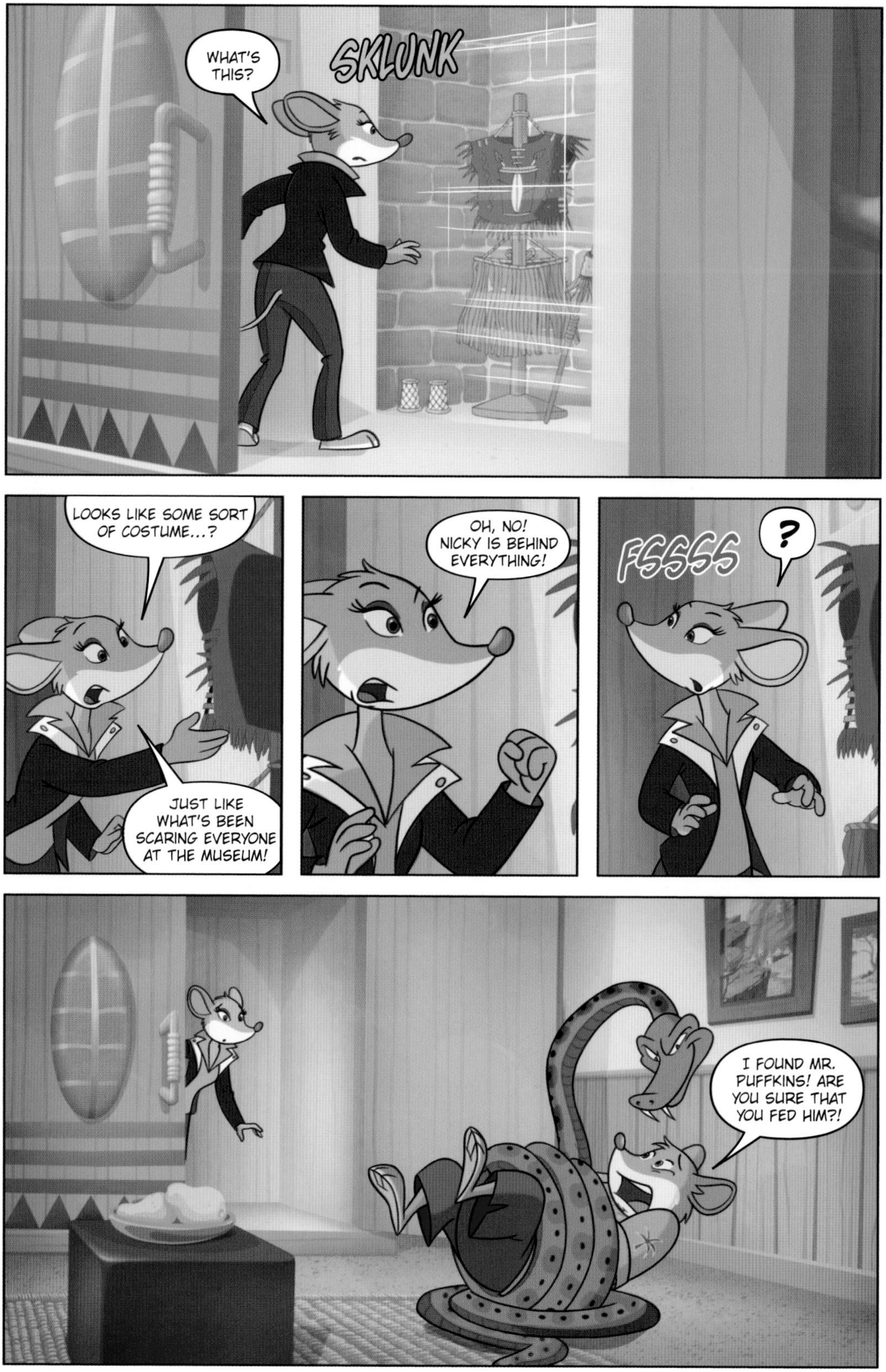
WHAT'S THIS?
SKLUNK
LOOKS LIKE SOME SORT OF COSTUME...?
JUST LIKE WHAT'S BEEN SCARING EVERYONE AT THE MUSEUM!
OH, NO! NICKY IS BEHIND EVERYTHING!
FSSSS
?
I FOUND MR. PUFFKINS! ARE YOU SURE THAT YOU FED HIM?!

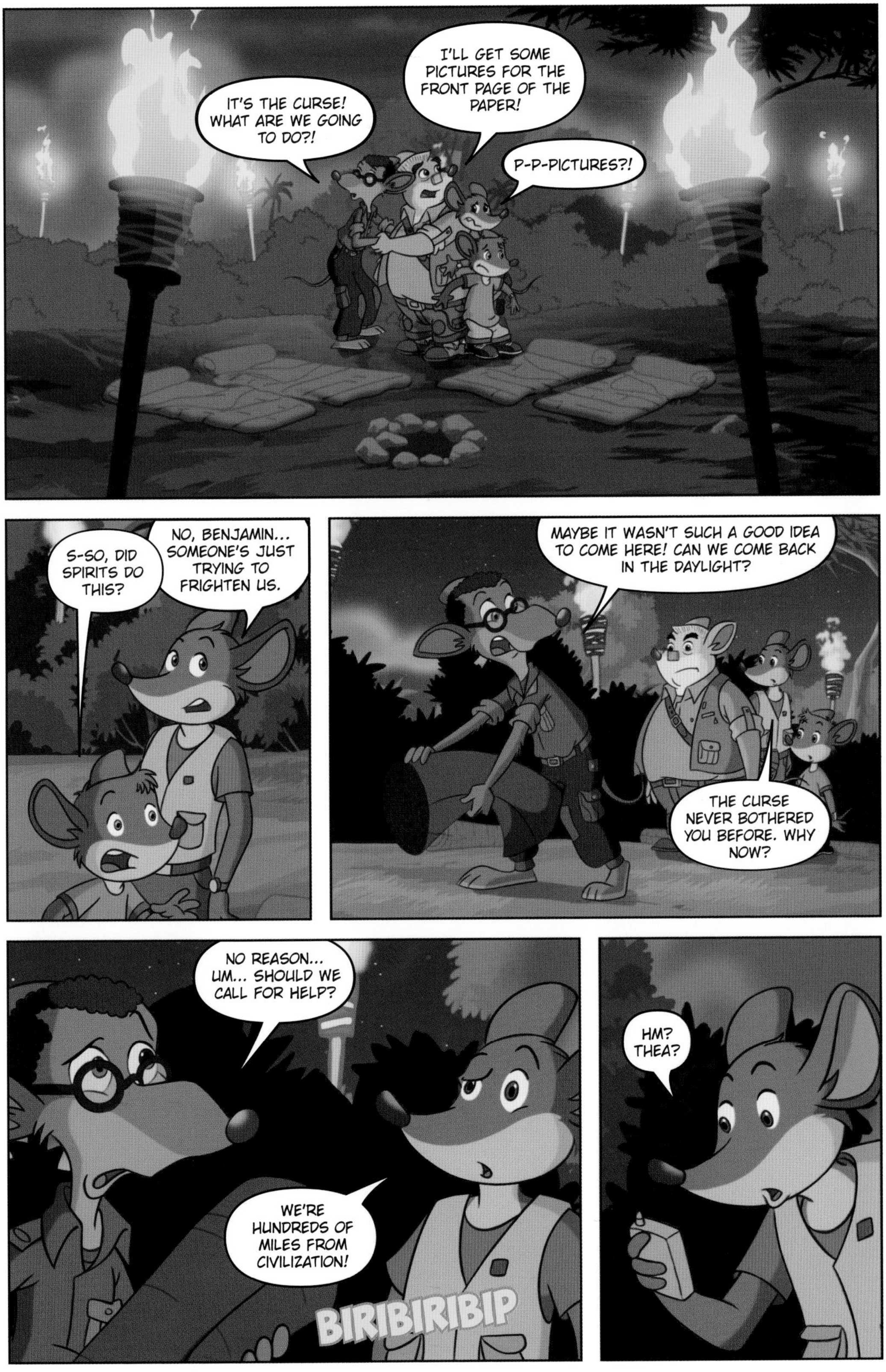
IT'S THE CURSE! WHAT ARE WE GOING TO DO?!
I'LL GET SOME PICTURES FOR THE FRONT PAGE OF THE PAPER!
P-P-PICTURES?!
S-SO, DID SPIRITS DO THIS?
NO, BENJAMIN... SOMEONE'S JUST TRYING TO FRIGHTEN US.
MAYBE IT WASN'T SUCH A GOOD IDEA TO COME HERE! CAN WE COME BACK IN THE DAYLIGHT?
THE CURSE NEVER BOTHERED YOU BEFORE. WHY NOW?
NO REASON... UM... SHOULD WE CALL FOR HELP?
WE'RE HUNDREDS OF MILES FROM CIVILIZATION!
BIRIBIRIBIP
HM? THEA?

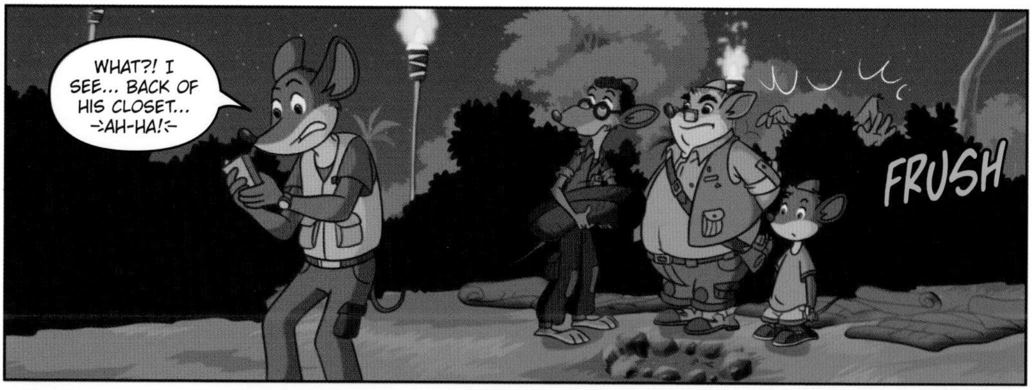
WHAT?! I SEE... BACK OF HIS CLOSET... -AH-HA!-
FRUSH

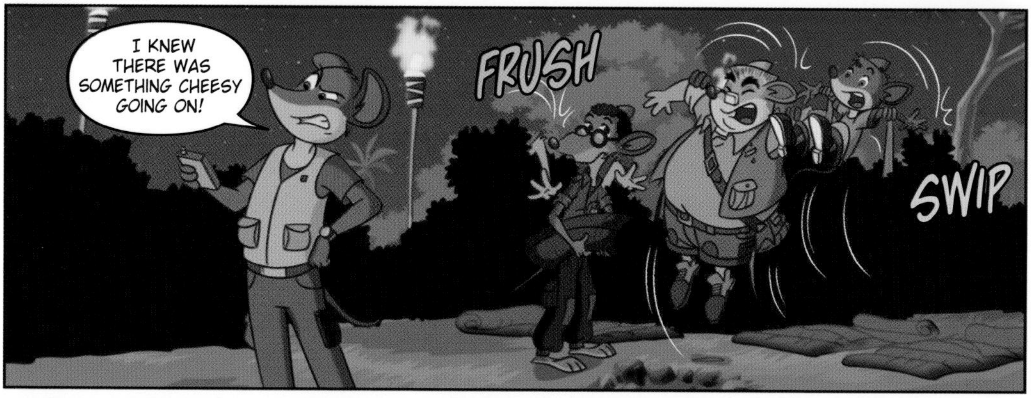
I KNEW THERE WAS SOMETHING CHEESY GOING ON!
FRUSH
SWIP

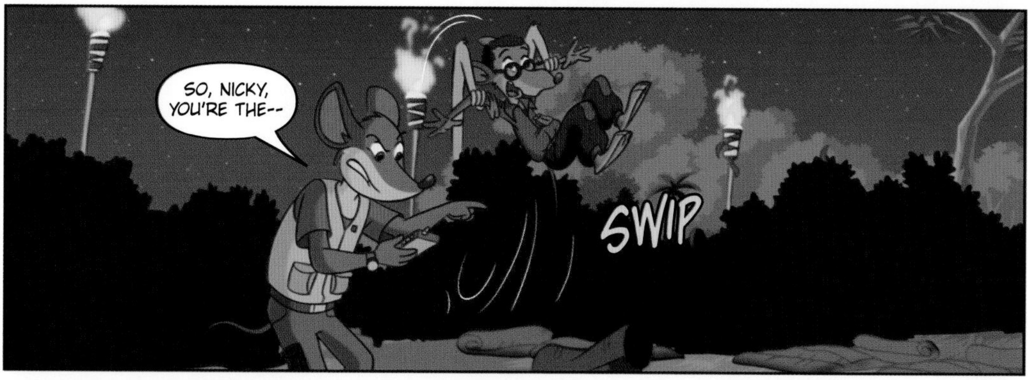
SO, NICKY, YOU'RE THE--
SWIP

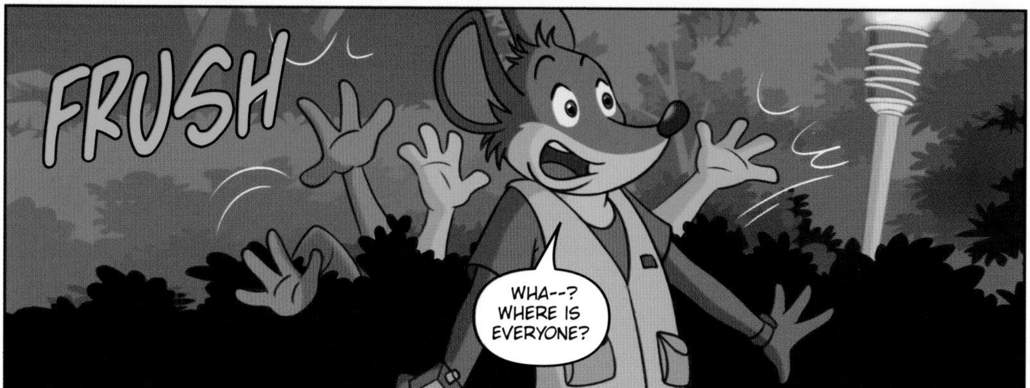
FRUSH
WHA--? WHERE IS EVERYONE?

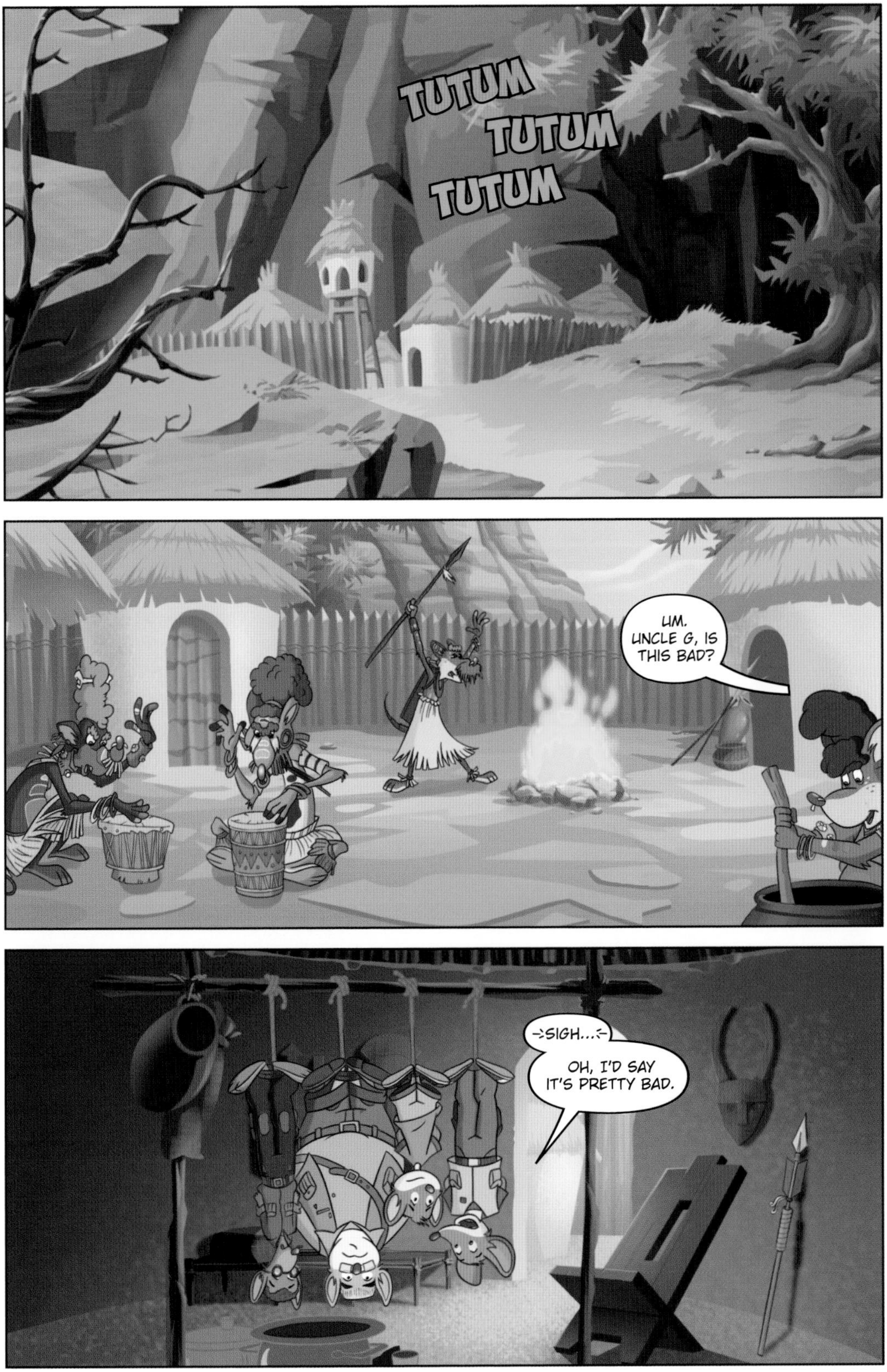
TUTUM
TUTUM
TUTUM
UM. UNCLE G, IS THIS BAD?
-SIGH...-
OH, I'D SAY IT'S PRETTY BAD.

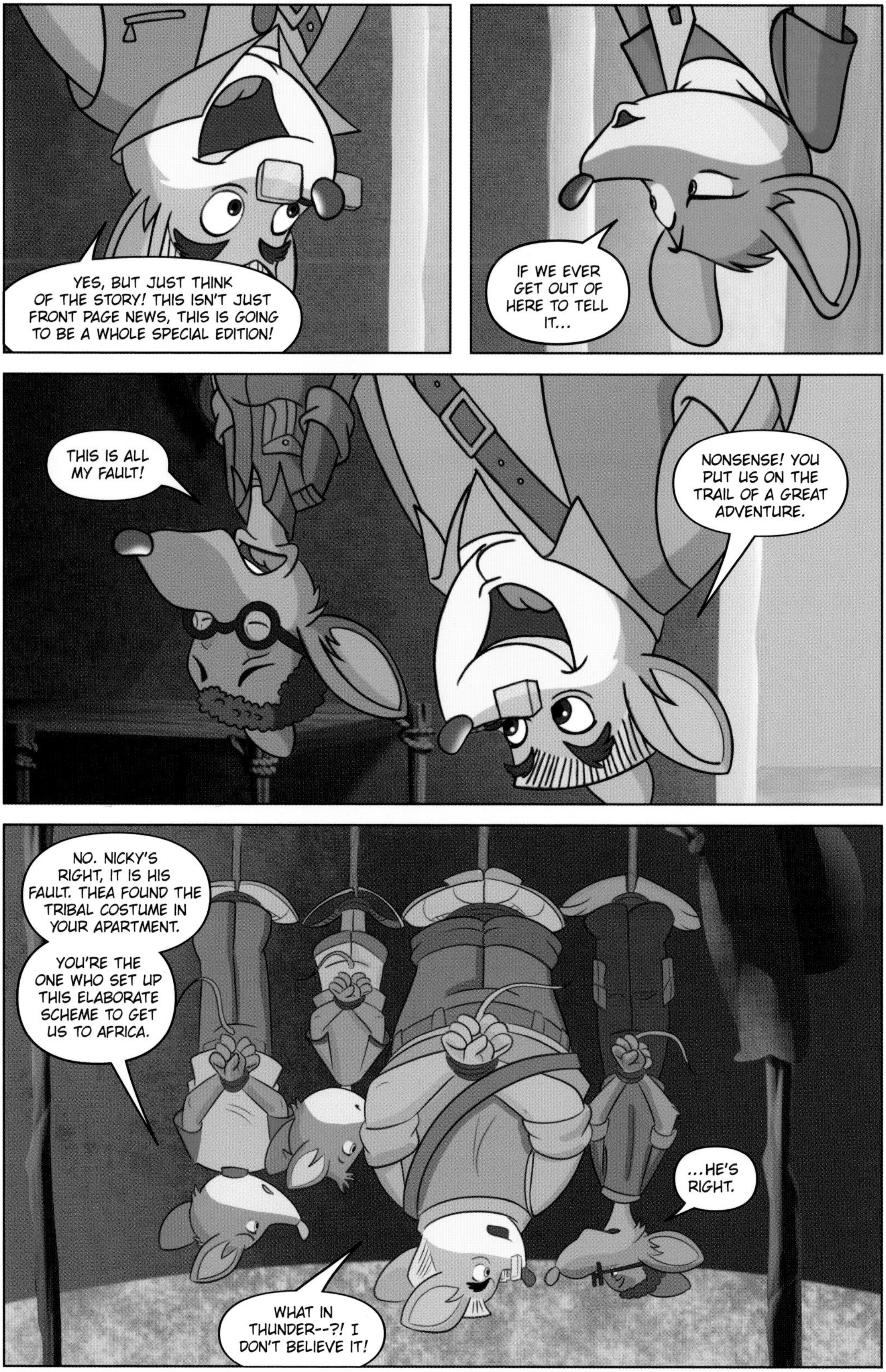
YES, BUT JUST THINK OF THE STORY! THIS ISN'T JUST FRONT PAGE NEWS, THIS IS GOING TO BE A WHOLE SPECIAL EDITION!
IF WE EVER GET OUT OF HERE TO TELL IT...
THIS IS ALL MY FAULT!
NONSENSE! YOU PUT US ON THE TRAIL OF A GREAT ADVENTURE.
NO. NICKY'S RIGHT, IT IS HIS FAULT. THEA FOUND THE TRIBAL COSTUME IN YOUR APARTMENT.
YOU'RE THE ONE WHO SET UP THIS ELABORATE SCHEME TO GET US TO AFRICA.
...HE'S RIGHT.
WHAT IN THUNDER--?! I DON'T BELIEVE IT!

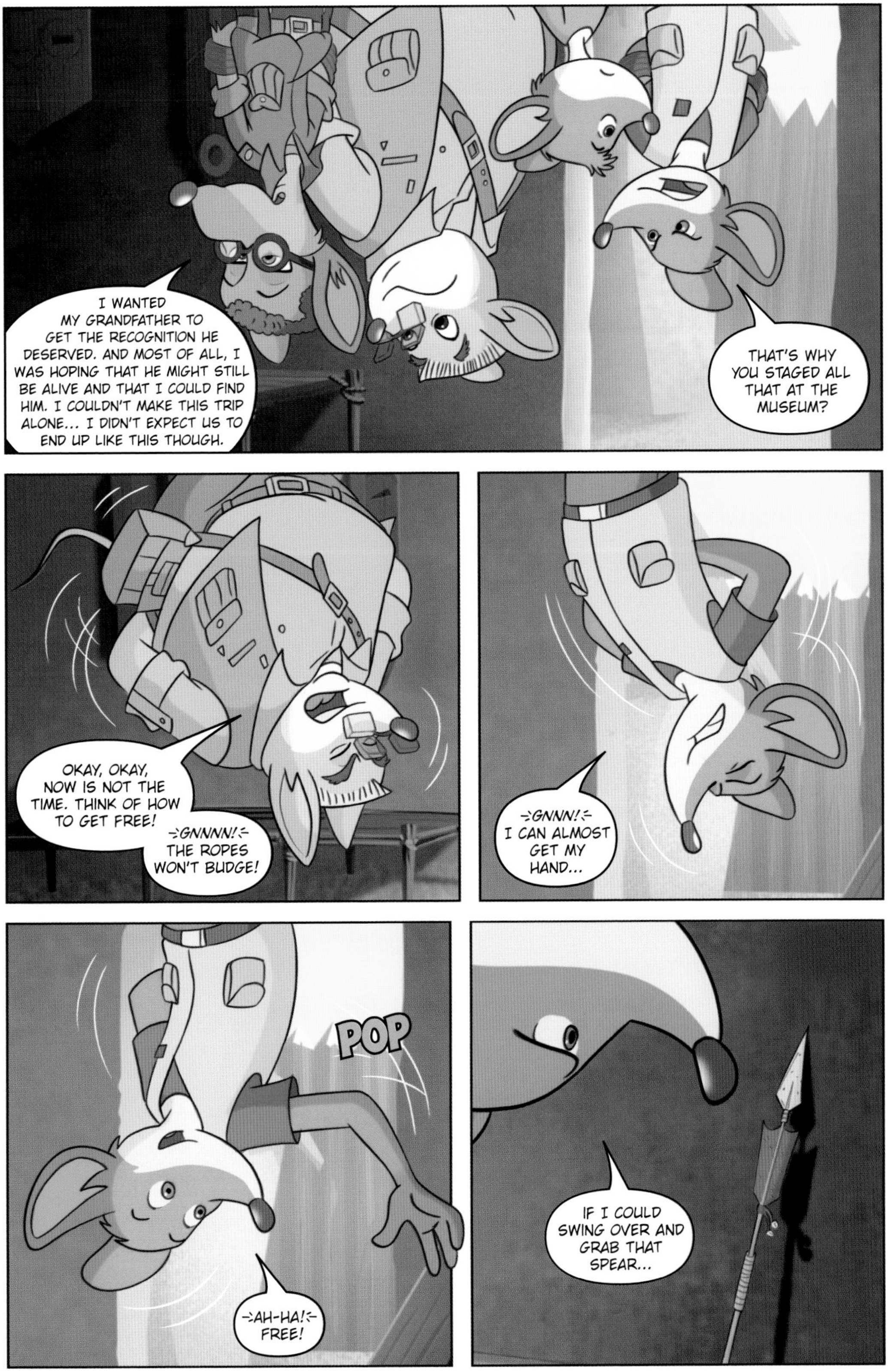
I WANTED MY GRANDFATHER TO GET THE RECOGNITION HE DESERVED. AND MOST OF ALL, I WAS HOPING THAT HE MIGHT STILL BE ALIVE AND THAT I COULD FIND HIM. I COULDN'T MAKE THIS TRIP ALONE... I DIDN'T EXPECT US TO END UP LIKE THIS THOUGH.
THAT'S WHY YOU STAGED ALL THAT AT THE MUSEUM?
OKAY, OKAY, NOW IS NOT THE TIME. THINK OF HOW TO GET FREE!
-GNNNN!- THE ROPES WON'T BUDGE!
-GNNN!- I CAN ALMOST GET MY HAND...
POP
-AH-HA!- FREE!
IF I COULD SWING OVER AND GRAB THAT SPEAR...

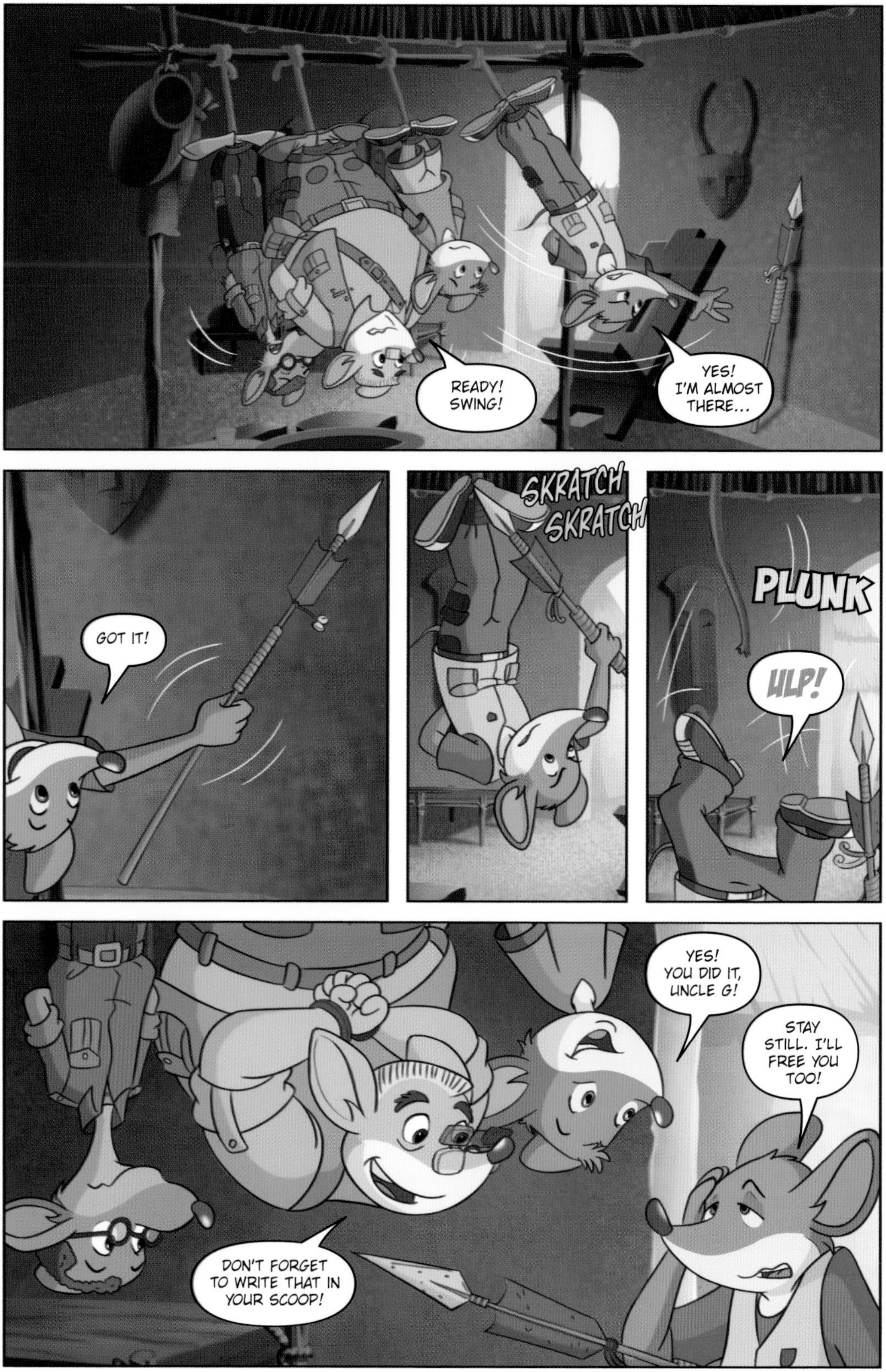
READY! SWING!
YES! I'M ALMOST THERE...
GOT IT!
SKRATCH SKRATCH
PLUNK
ULP!
YES! YOU DID IT, UNCLE G!
STAY STILL. I'LL FREE YOU TOO!
DON'T FORGET TO WRITE THAT IN YOUR SCOOP!

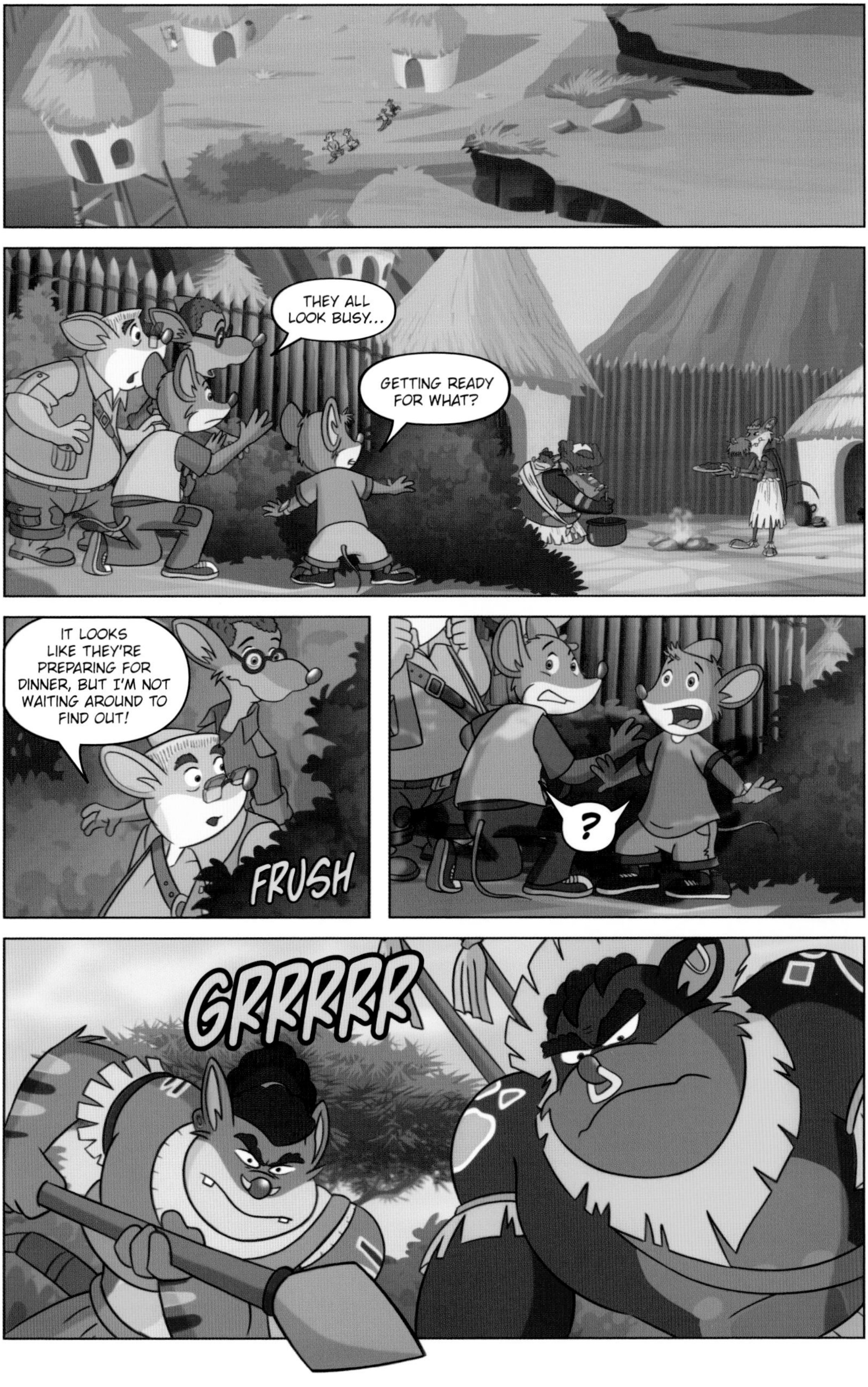
THEY ALL LOOK BUSY...
GETTING READY FOR WHAT?
IT LOOKS LIKE THEY'RE PREPARING FOR DINNER, BUT I'M NOT WAITING AROUND TO FIND OUT!
FRUSH
?
GRRRRR

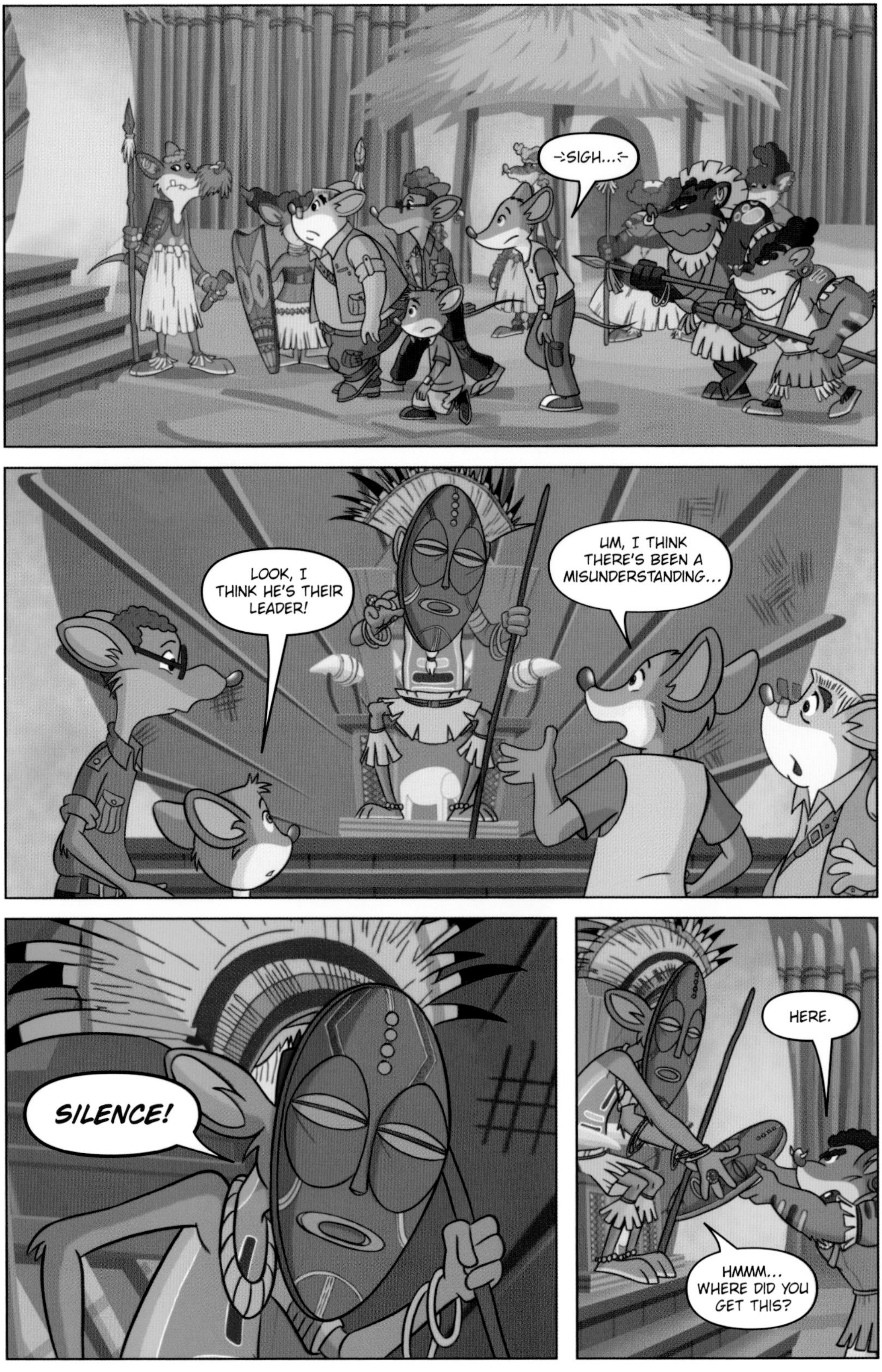
SIGH...
LOOK, I THINK HE'S THEIR LEADER!
UM, I THINK THERE'S BEEN A MISUNDERSTANDING...
SILENCE!
HERE.
HMMM... WHERE DID YOU GET THIS?

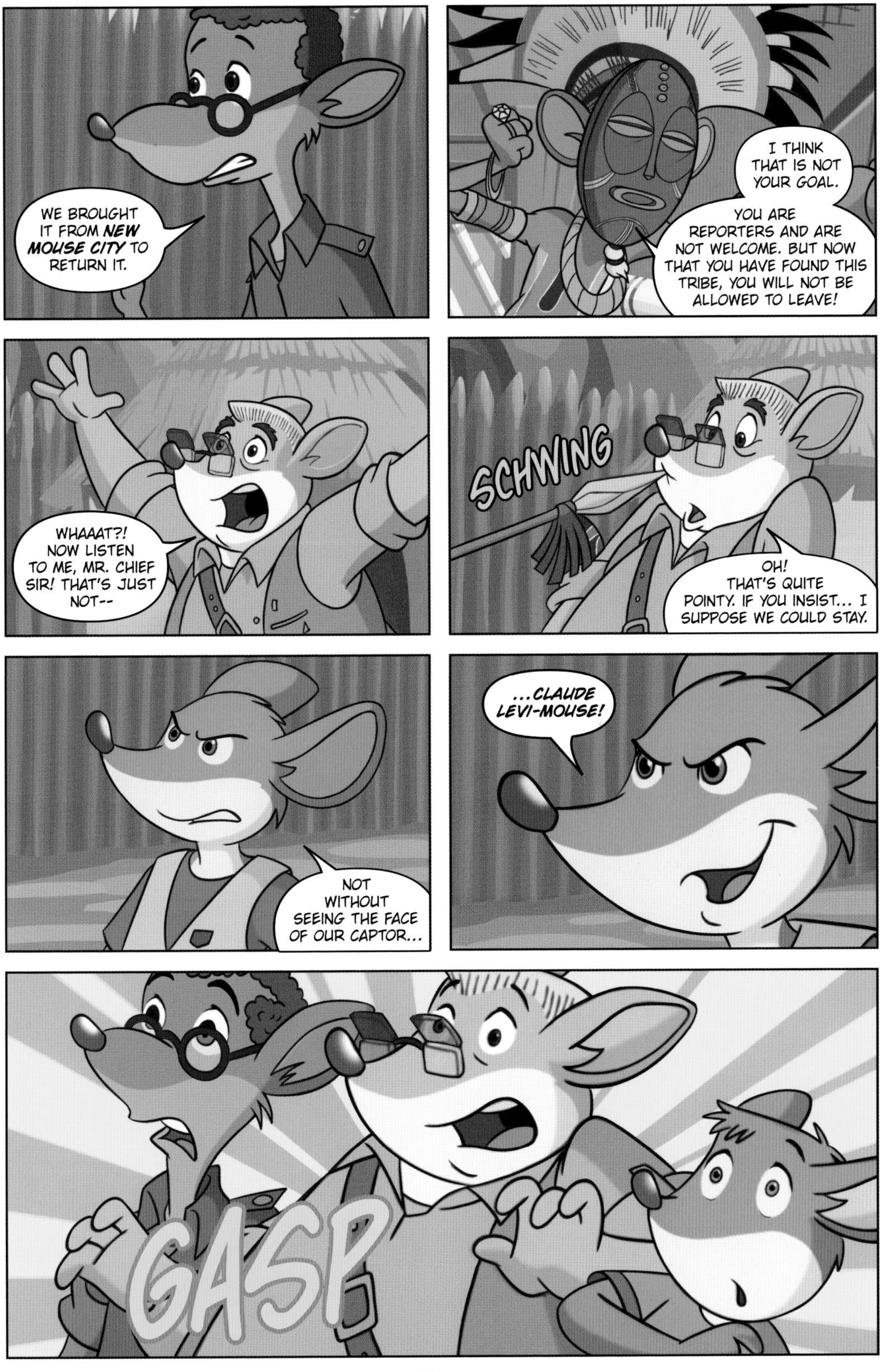
WE BROUGHT IT FROM **NEW MOUSE CITY** TO RETURN IT.
I THINK THAT IS NOT YOUR GOAL.
YOU ARE REPORTERS AND ARE NOT WELCOME. BUT NOW THAT YOU HAVE FOUND THIS TRIBE, YOU WILL NOT BE ALLOWED TO LEAVE!
WHAAAT?! NOW LISTEN TO ME, MR. CHIEF SIR! THAT'S JUST NOT--
SCHWING
OH! THAT'S QUITE POINTY. IF YOU INSIST... I SUPPOSE WE COULD STAY.
NOT WITHOUT SEEING THE FACE OF OUR CAPTOR...
...CLAUDE LEVI-MOUSE!
GASP

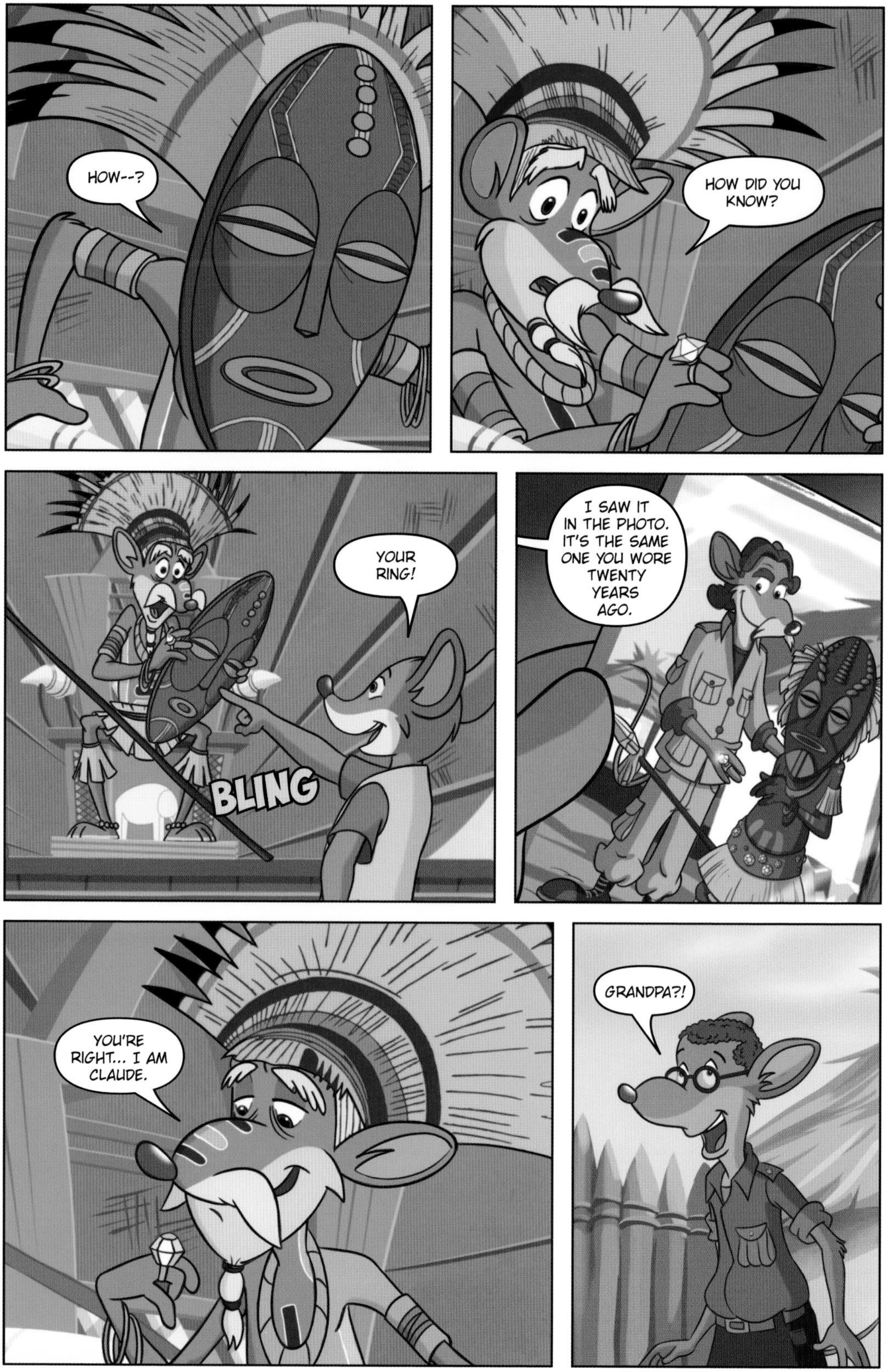
HOW--?
HOW DID YOU KNOW?
YOUR RING!
BLING
I SAW IT IN THE PHOTO. IT'S THE SAME ONE YOU WORE TWENTY YEARS AGO.
YOU'RE RIGHT... I AM CLAUDE.
GRANDPA?!

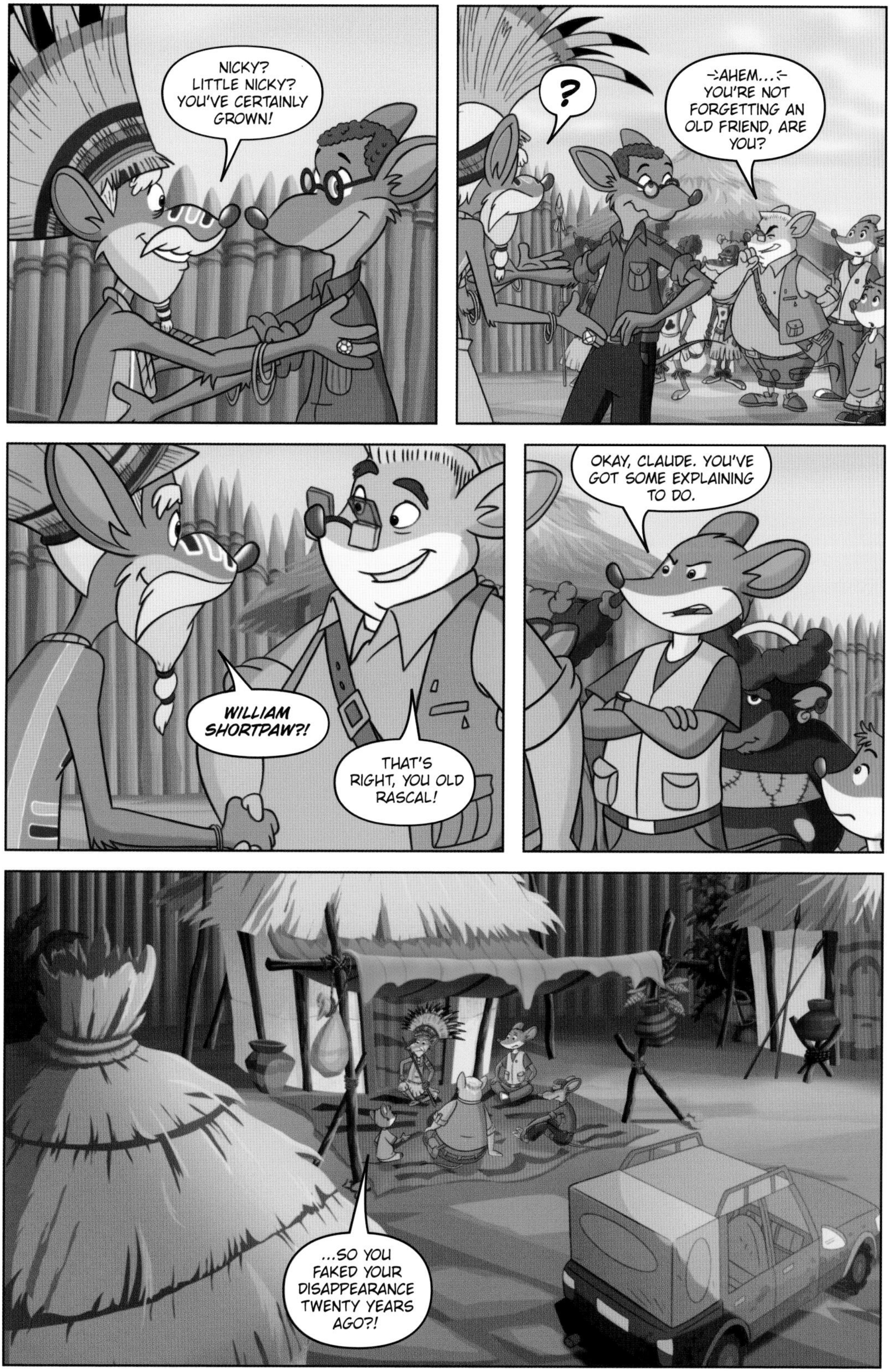
NICKY? LITTLE NICKY? YOU'VE CERTAINLY GROWN!
?
AHEM... YOU'RE NOT FORGETTING AN OLD FRIEND, ARE YOU?
WILLIAM SHORTPAW?!
THAT'S RIGHT, YOU OLD RASCAL!
OKAY, CLAUDE. YOU'VE GOT SOME EXPLAINING TO DO.
...SO YOU FAKED YOUR DISAPPEARANCE TWENTY YEARS AGO?!

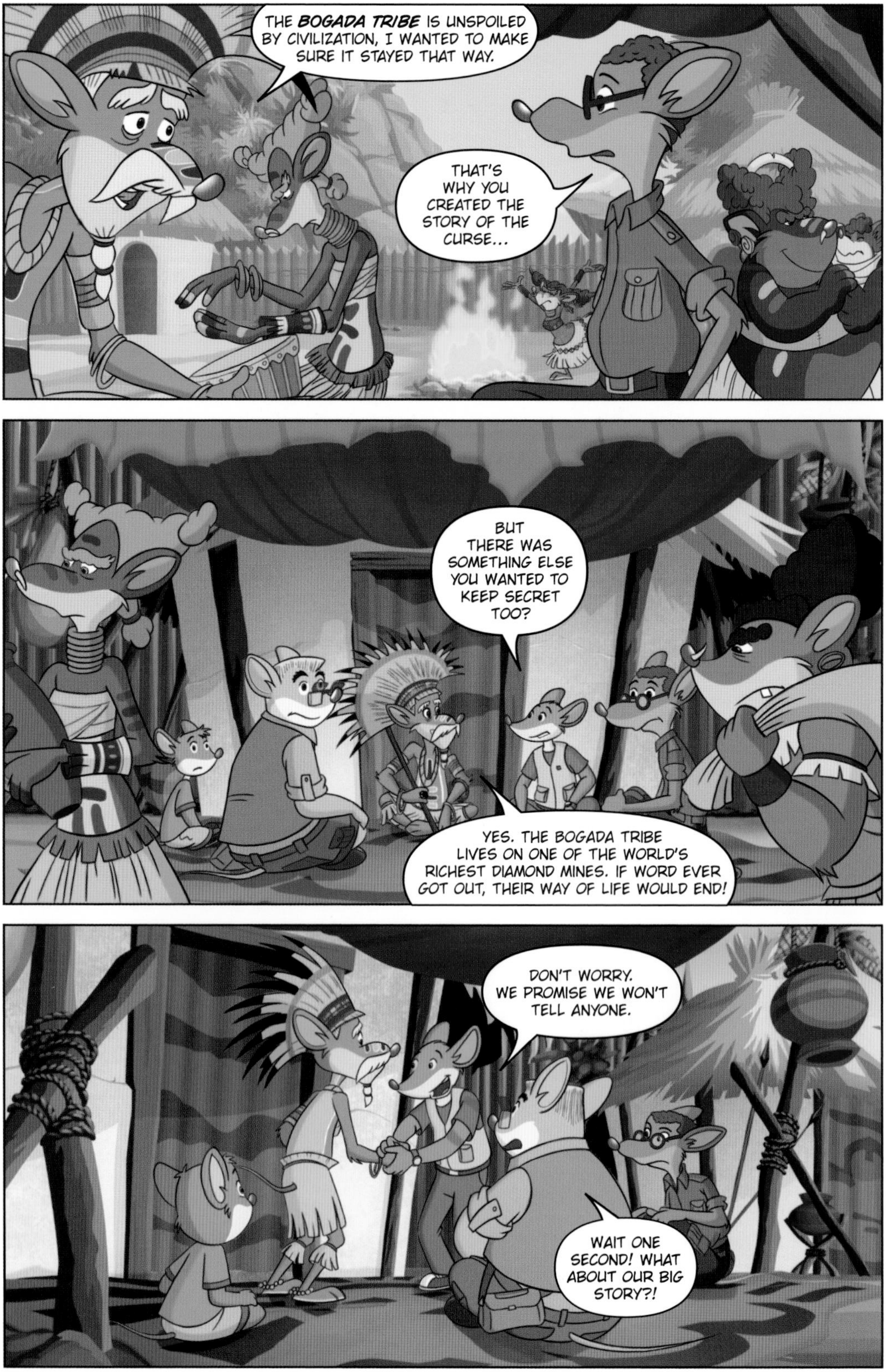
THE BOGADA TRIBE IS UNSPOILED BY CIVILIZATION, I WANTED TO MAKE SURE IT STAYED THAT WAY.
THAT'S WHY YOU CREATED THE STORY OF THE CURSE...
BUT THERE WAS SOMETHING ELSE YOU WANTED TO KEEP SECRET TOO?
YES. THE BOGADA TRIBE LIVES ON ONE OF THE WORLD'S RICHEST DIAMOND MINES. IF WORD EVER GOT OUT, THEIR WAY OF LIFE WOULD END!
DON'T WORRY. WE PROMISE WE WON'T TELL ANYONE.
WAIT ONE SECOND! WHAT ABOUT OUR BIG STORY?!

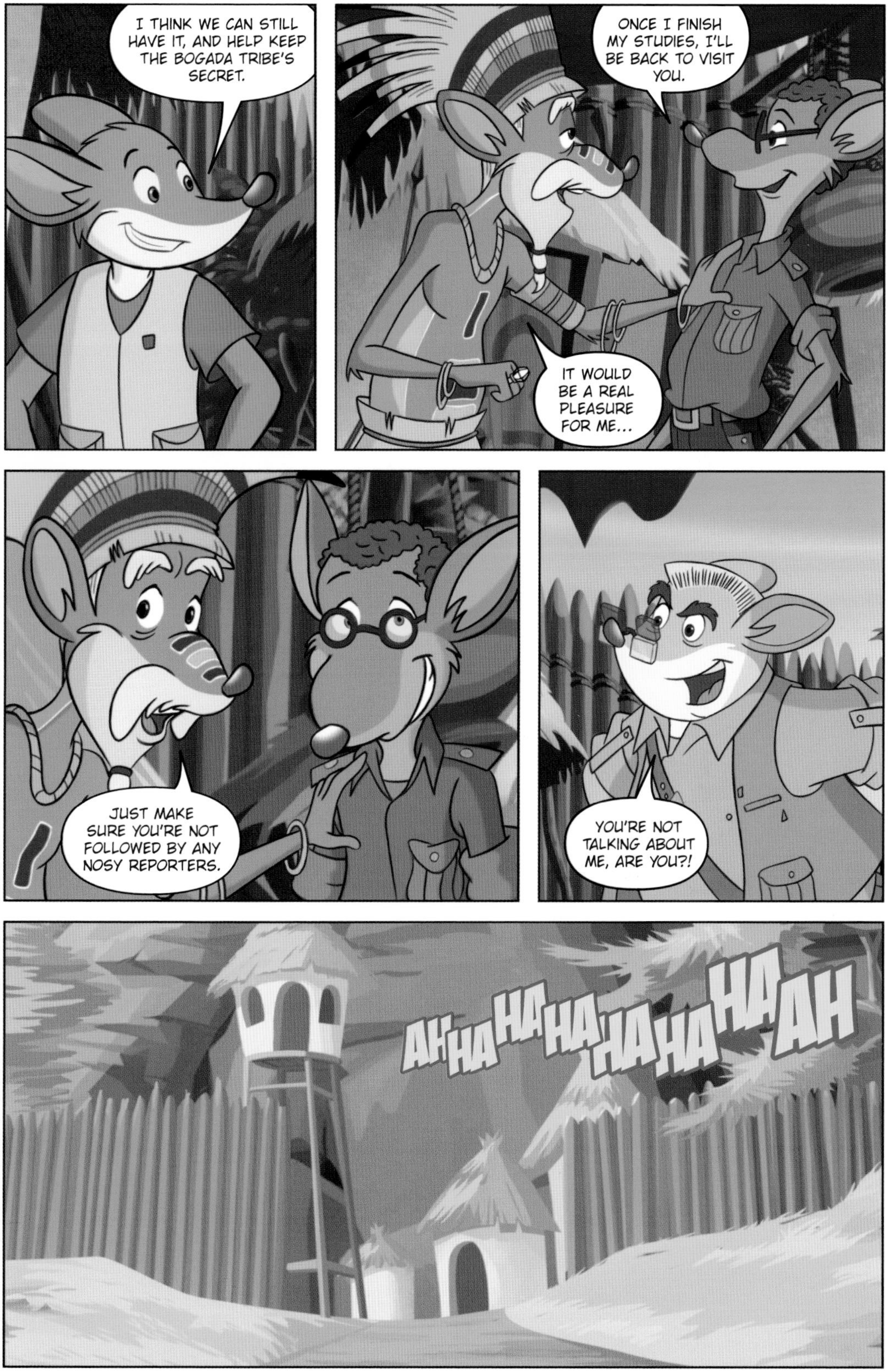
I THINK WE CAN STILL HAVE IT, AND HELP KEEP THE BOGADA TRIBE'S SECRET.
ONCE I FINISH MY STUDIES, I'LL BE BACK TO VISIT YOU.
IT WOULD BE A REAL PLEASURE FOR ME...
JUST MAKE SURE YOU'RE NOT FOLLOWED BY ANY NOSY REPORTERS.
YOU'RE NOT TALKING ABOUT ME, ARE YOU?!
AHHAHAHAHAHAHAAH

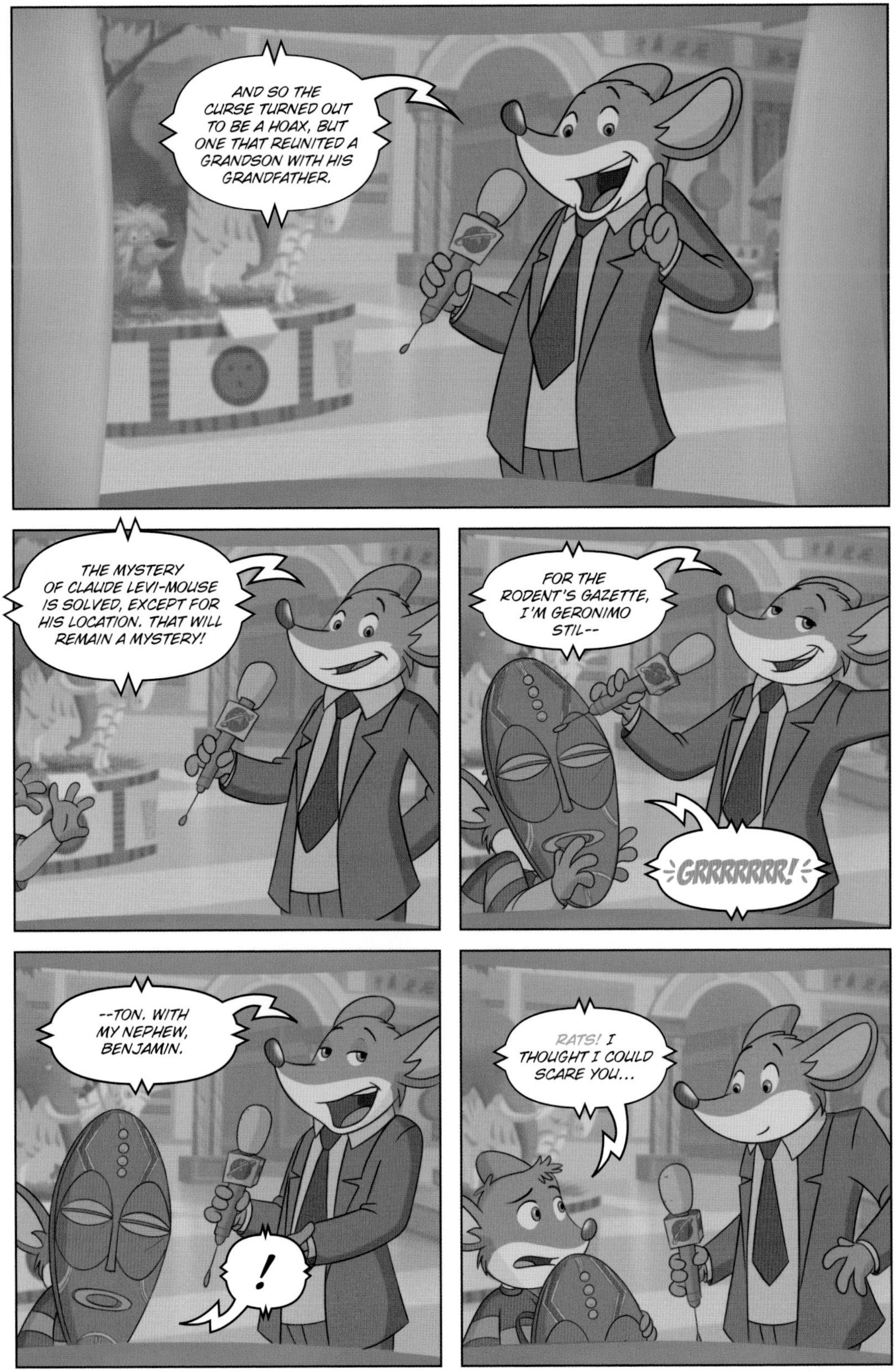
AND SO THE CURSE TURNED OUT TO BE A HOAX, BUT ONE THAT REUNITED A GRANDSON WITH HIS GRANDFATHER.
THE MYSTERY OF CLAUDE LEVI-MOUSE IS SOLVED, EXCEPT FOR HIS LOCATION. THAT WILL REMAIN A MYSTERY!
FOR THE RODENT'S GAZETTE, I'M GERONIMO STIL--
GRRRRRRR!
--TON. WITH MY NEPHEW, BENJAMIN.
!
RATS! I THOUGHT I COULD SCARE YOU...

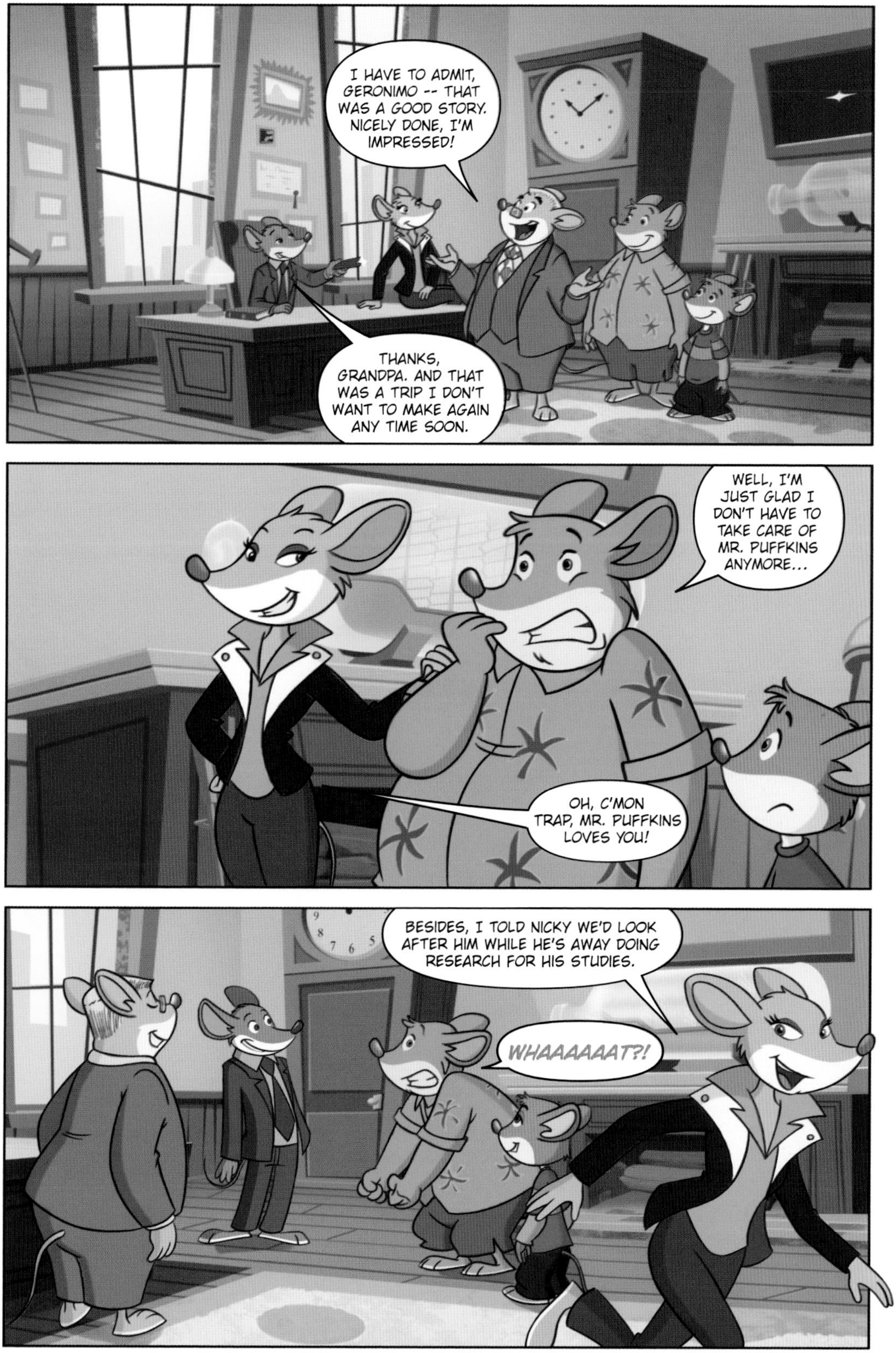
I HAVE TO ADMIT, GERONIMO -- THAT WAS A GOOD STORY. NICELY DONE, I'M IMPRESSED!
THANKS, GRANDPA. AND THAT WAS A TRIP I DON'T WANT TO MAKE AGAIN ANY TIME SOON.
WELL, I'M JUST GLAD I DON'T HAVE TO TAKE CARE OF MR. PUFFKINS ANYMORE...
OH, C'MON TRAP, MR. PUFFKINS LOVES YOU!
BESIDES, I TOLD NICKY WE'D LOOK AFTER HIM WHILE HE'S AWAY DOING RESEARCH FOR HIS STUDIES.
WHAAAAAAT?!

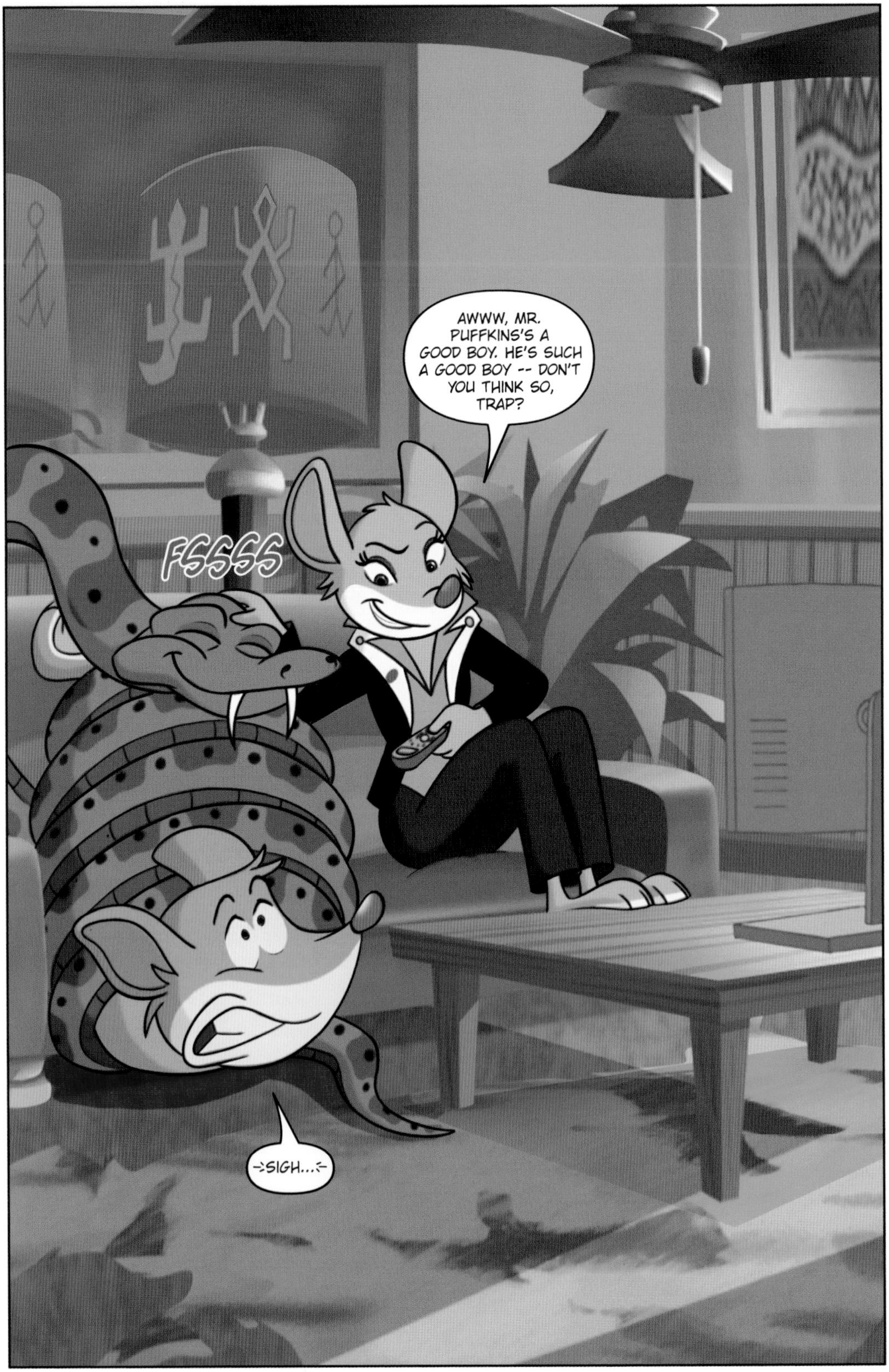
AWWW, MR. PUFFKINS'S A GOOD BOY. HE'S SUCH A GOOD BOY -- DON'T YOU THINK SO, TRAP?
FSSSS
SIGH...

Watch Out For PAPERCUTZ

"Hello, I Must Be Going." –sung by Groucho Marx as Captain Spaulding in the 1930 film, Animal Crackers

Welcome to the lucky thirteenth GERONIMO STILTON REPORTER graphic novel, "Reported Missing," the official comics adaptation of the animated *Geronimo Stilton* TV series, Season One, Episode 13, written by Catherine Cuenca and Patrick Regnard, brought to you by Papercutz—those remotely-working folks dedicated to publishing great graphic novels for all ages. I'm *Jim Salicrup*, the soon-to-be erstwhile Editor-in-Chief and Locator of Lost Pencils, here to share some really big Papercutz news…

While I'm sure our friend, Geronimo Stilton, would've loved getting the scoop on this story, alas, it was already reported on Forbes.com that Papercutz has been purchased by Mad Cave Studios. This is great news, as it means Papercutz will not only continue to bring you the graphic novels you already love, but will also launch even more. And Mad Cave Studios has the resources to do an even better job of promoting and marketing Papercutz and getting our graphic novels onto the shelves of even more booksellers and libraries, both print and digital editions. The new Papercutz Editorial Director is Rex Ogle, who has worked at Marvel and DC Comics, as well as Scholastic and Little Brown for Young Readers. He's worked on everything from *LEGO* and *Minecraft* to *Star Wars* and *Buffy the Vampire Slayer*. When he's not editing books, he's either reading or writing them. Joining Rex will be Senior Editor Zohra Ashpari, who was previously an editor at Tapas Media and has worked within the editorial departments of Scholastic and Tor Books. And completing the new editorial team will be Assistant Editor Stephanie Brooks, who started as an editorial intern at NBM before becoming my Assistant Managing Editor at Papercutz. Welcome, Rex, Zohra, and Stephanie! The future of Papercutz is certainly in good hands!

Over twenty years ago, graphic novel pioneer and NBM publisher, Terry Nantier, had the brilliant concept of starting yet another graphic novel publishing company. When he originally launched NBM, the idea of comics for adults was revolutionary in the United States. After successfully proving that concept could succeed, he noticed that almost every comics publisher was then aiming their comics to the adult audience, virtually abandoning kids. That's when Terry realized that there should be comics for kids again, especially for girls, and the idea for Papercutz was born. The name Papercutz was dreamed up by Terry's daughter Sylvia, who specifically requested that it not be spelled with a Z at the end, but you know how dads can be. That's also around the time that Terry asked me to be his partner and Editor-in-Chief in this crazy new venture, for which I readily agreed. I had started at Marvel Comics in 1972 when I was fifteen years old (This year marks my 50th anniversary of working in comics!). The year before that I was one of the kids at Kid's Magazine. Seems I've always been interested in comics for kids. Even at Marvel I had written and then edited SPIDEY SUPER STORIES, a kids version of Spider-Man comics designed to help children read, co-produced with the producers of Sesame Street and The Electric Company, the Children's Television Workshop. And there were many other kids-oriented projects that I worked on over the years.

The first Papercutz comicbook, THE HARDY BOYS, was published in 2004, and in 2005, the first Papercutz graphic novels, THE HARDY BOYS and NANCY DREW saw print. And we've been at it ever since, through a world-wide Great Recession in 2008 and the recent global Covid Pandemic. But after almost twenty years Terry and I decided it was time for others to take Papercutz up to the next level, and that's where Mad Cave Studios comes in. While there was virtually no competition in the kids graphic novel category when we started, now almost every comics and book publisher is producing graphic novels for kids. Mad Cave Studios is better equipped to handle that kind of fierce competition.

For Terry and me, it's a little like Papercutz is one of our children that has grown up and is going off to college. While we both will still be around for another 8 months as consultants to make the transition go as smoothly as possible, eventually we'll be moving on, leaving our baby in the very capable hands of Mad Cave Studios. While I may be leaving Papercutz, I'm certainly not leaving comics. There've been may other projects I've been hoping to work on, but Papercutz had been taking up almost every waking hour of my time. Now I'll be free to work on those projects.

There are way too many people I'd like to thank for making my time at Papercutz over the years so wonderful. Terry, of course, the best publishing partner I could ever imagine! All of our writers, artists, letterers, colorists, production people, and of course, my invaluable, hard-working Managing Editors Michael Petranek, Bethany Bryan, Suzannah Rowntree, Jeff Whitman, and Stephanie Brooks. And of course, all of you, the Papercutz fans who have supported us over the years, with a special shout out to Rachel Boden, one of our biggest fans.

One truly sad note. We'd also like to take a moment to acknowledge the passing of NANCY DREW GIRL DETECTIVE artist Sho Murase (1969-2022). Sho was the artist on what was one of Papercutz's first graphic novels and continued on that series for most of the volumes. She was an incredibly talented artist and a wonderful human being. Her totally modern, manga-influenced style played a big role in making that series such a big success and well-loved by its fans. We miss her dearly.

On the bright side, GERONIMO STILTON REPORTER will be back soon, in his 14th graphic novel, "The Gem Gang." Take a look at the preview on the following pages. We also have a bonus excerpt from the most recent volume of MELOWY. What's a MELOWY? Pretty much a female flying unicorn, and this series features an entire school of them. This bonus excerpt follows directly after the GERONIMO STILTON REPORTER preview.

This will also be the final *Watch Out for Papercutz* column in GERONIMO STILTON REPORTER, but in light of the great news regarding Mad Cave Studios taking over, may my last words simply be, *watch out for Papercutz*—the best is yet to come!

Thanks,

Jim

Steal a quick peek of the Special Preview for GERONIMO STILTON REPORTER Graphic Novel #14 "THE GEM GANG"

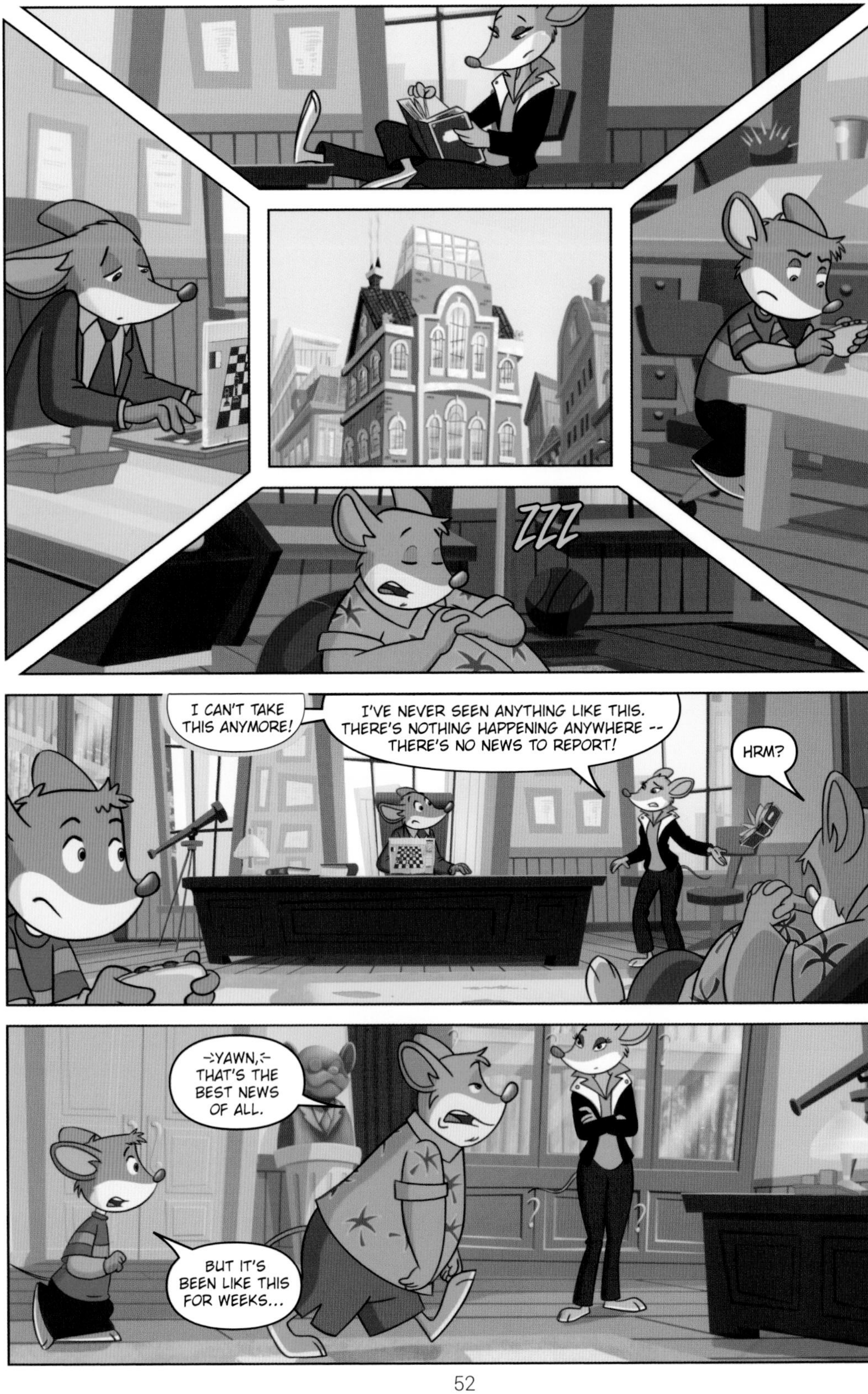
ZZZ
I CAN'T TAKE THIS ANYMORE!
I'VE NEVER SEEN ANYTHING LIKE THIS. THERE'S NOTHING HAPPENING ANYWHERE -- THERE'S NO NEWS TO REPORT!
HRM?
YAWN, THAT'S THE BEST NEWS OF ALL.
BUT IT'S BEEN LIKE THIS FOR WEEKS...

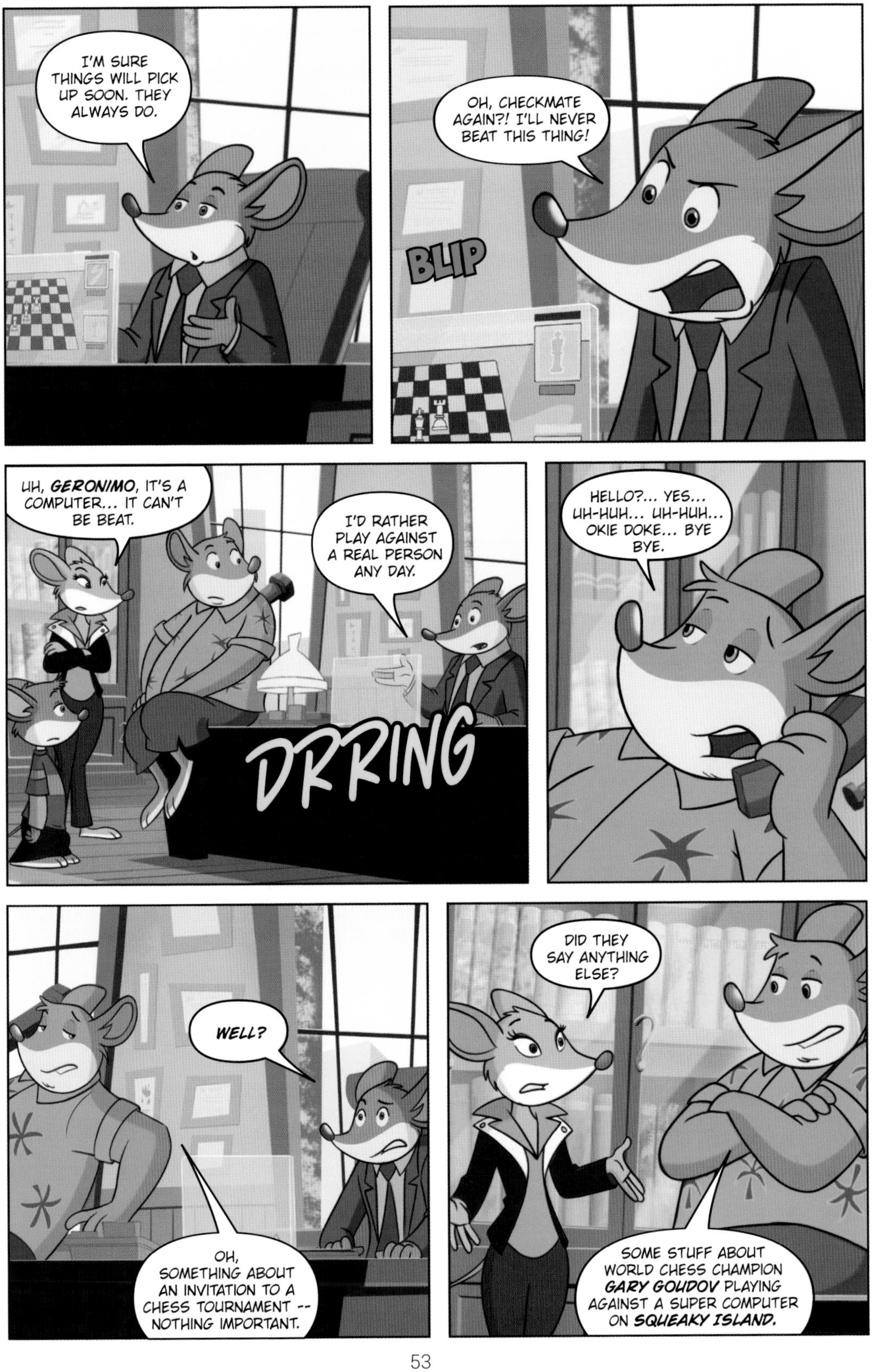
I'M SURE THINGS WILL PICK UP SOON. THEY ALWAYS DO.
OH, CHECKMATE AGAIN?! I'LL NEVER BEAT THIS THING!
BLIP
UH, GERONIMO, IT'S A COMPUTER... IT CAN'T BE BEAT.
I'D RATHER PLAY AGAINST A REAL PERSON ANY DAY.
DRRING
HELLO?... YES... UH-HUH... UH-HUH... OKIE DOKE... BYE BYE.
WELL?
OH, SOMETHING ABOUT AN INVITATION TO A CHESS TOURNAMENT -- NOTHING IMPORTANT.
DID THEY SAY ANYTHING ELSE?
SOME STUFF ABOUT WORLD CHESS CHAMPION GARY GOUDOV PLAYING AGAINST A SUPER COMPUTER ON SQUEAKY ISLAND.

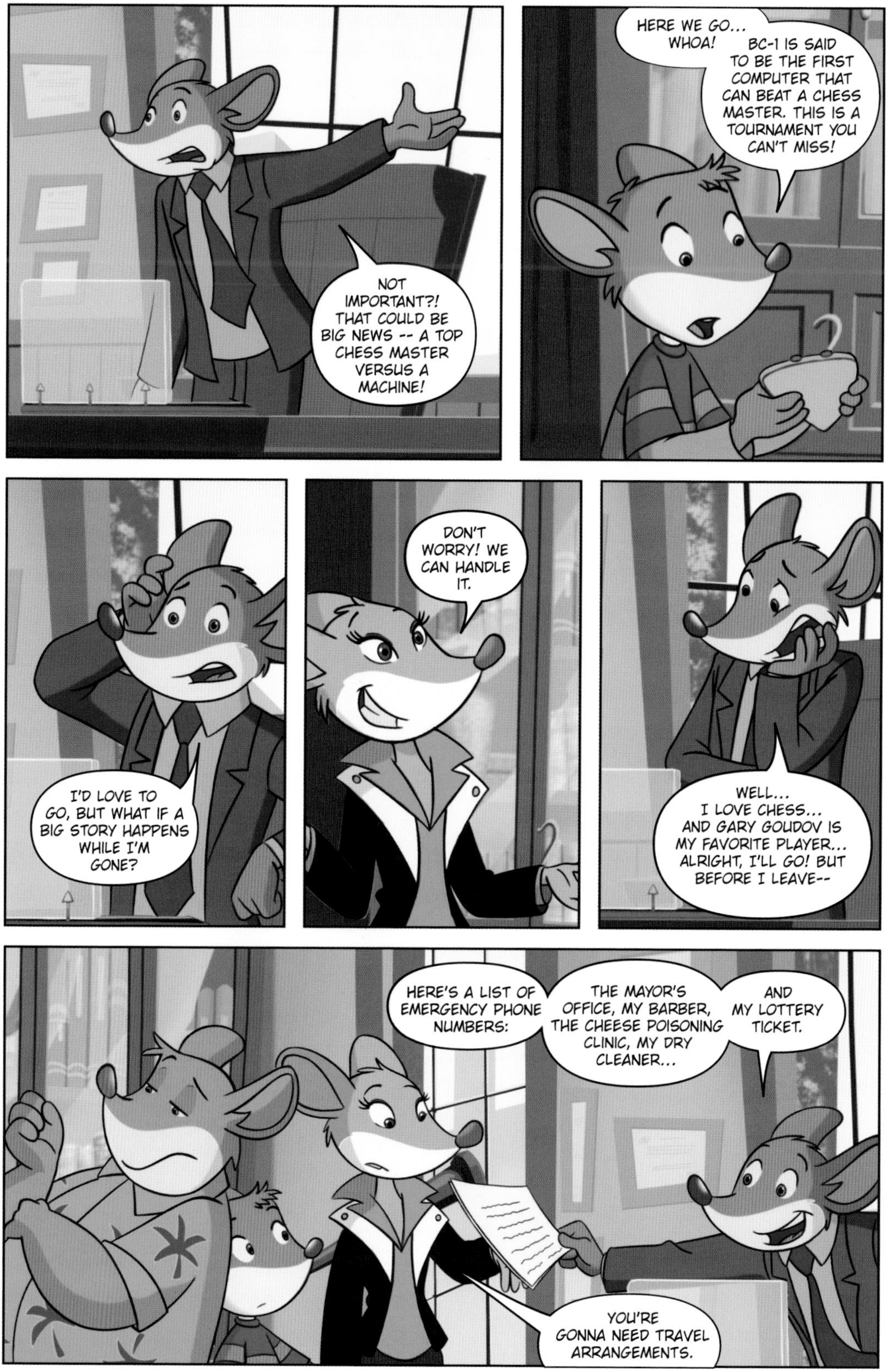
NOT IMPORTANT?! THAT COULD BE BIG NEWS -- A TOP CHESS MASTER VERSUS A MACHINE!
HERE WE GO... WHOA!
BC-1 IS SAID TO BE THE FIRST COMPUTER THAT CAN BEAT A CHESS MASTER. THIS IS A TOURNAMENT YOU CAN'T MISS!
I'D LOVE TO GO, BUT WHAT IF A BIG STORY HAPPENS WHILE I'M GONE?
DON'T WORRY! WE CAN HANDLE IT.
WELL... I LOVE CHESS... AND GARY GOUDOV IS MY FAVORITE PLAYER... ALRIGHT, I'LL GO! BUT BEFORE I LEAVE--
HERE'S A LIST OF EMERGENCY PHONE NUMBERS:
THE MAYOR'S OFFICE, MY BARBER, THE CHEESE POISONING CLINIC, MY DRY CLEANER...
AND MY LOTTERY TICKET.
YOU'RE GONNA NEED TRAVEL ARRANGEMENTS.

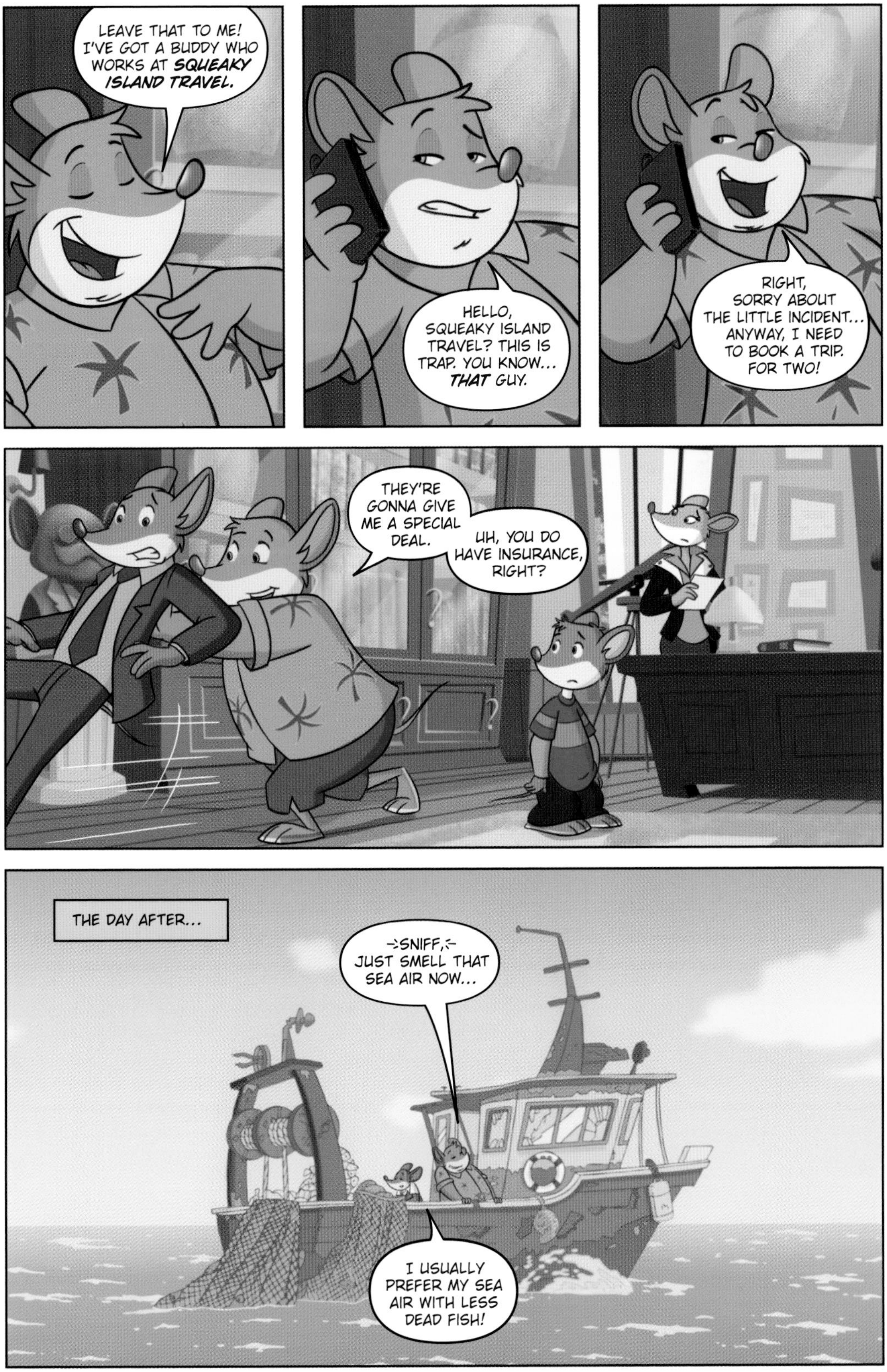
LEAVE THAT TO ME! I'VE GOT A BUDDY WHO WORKS AT **SQUEAKY ISLAND TRAVEL.**
HELLO, SQUEAKY ISLAND TRAVEL? THIS IS TRAP. YOU KNOW... ***THAT*** GUY.
RIGHT, SORRY ABOUT THE LITTLE INCIDENT... ANYWAY, I NEED TO BOOK A TRIP. FOR TWO!
THEY'RE GONNA GIVE ME A SPECIAL DEAL.
UH, YOU DO HAVE INSURANCE, RIGHT?
THE DAY AFTER...
SNIFF, JUST SMELL THAT SEA AIR NOW...
I USUALLY PREFER MY SEA AIR WITH LESS DEAD FISH!

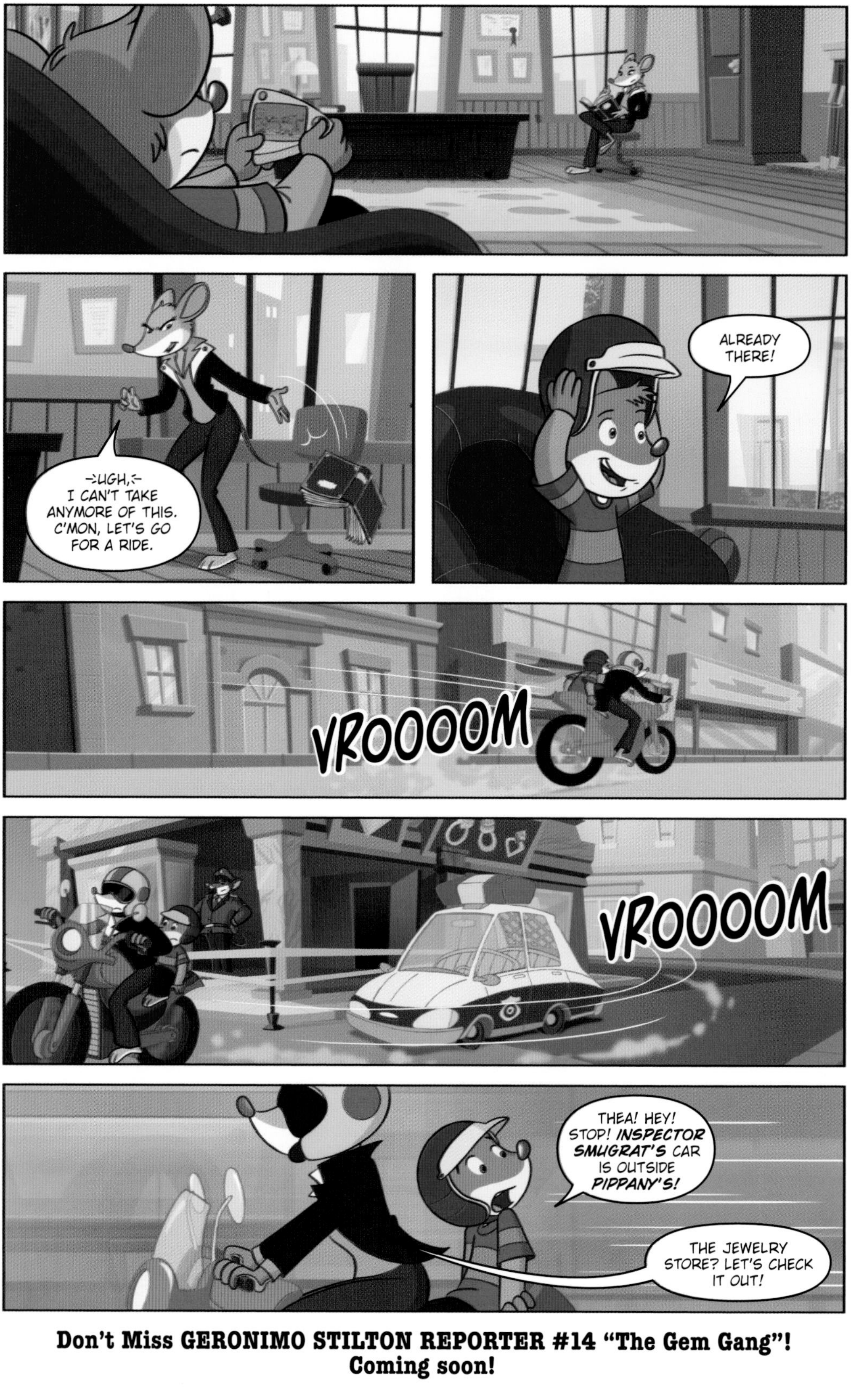
UGH,
I CAN'T TAKE ANYMORE OF THIS. C'MON, LET'S GO FOR A RIDE.
ALREADY THERE!
VROOOOM
VROOOOM
THEA! HEY! STOP! ***INSPECTOR SMUGRAT'S*** CAR IS OUTSIDE ***PIPPANY'S!***
THE JEWELRY STORE? LET'S CHECK IT OUT!

Don't Miss GERONIMO STILTON REPORTER #14 "The Gem Gang"!
Coming soon!

Here's an exclusive peek at MELOWY #5 "Meloween"...

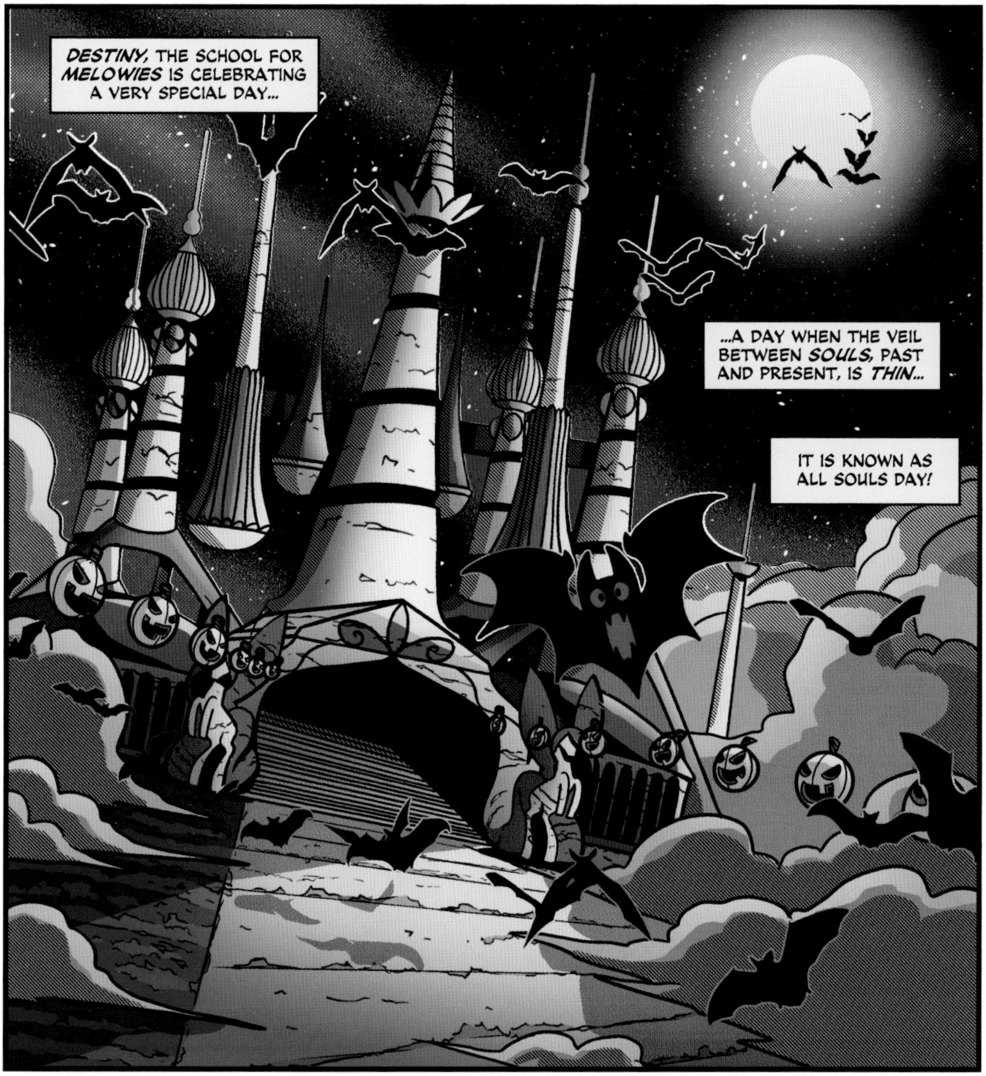
DESTINY, THE SCHOOL FOR MELOWIES IS CELEBRATING A VERY SPECIAL DAY...
...A DAY WHEN THE VEIL BETWEEN SOULS, PAST AND PRESENT, IS THIN...
IT IS KNOWN AS ALL SOULS DAY!

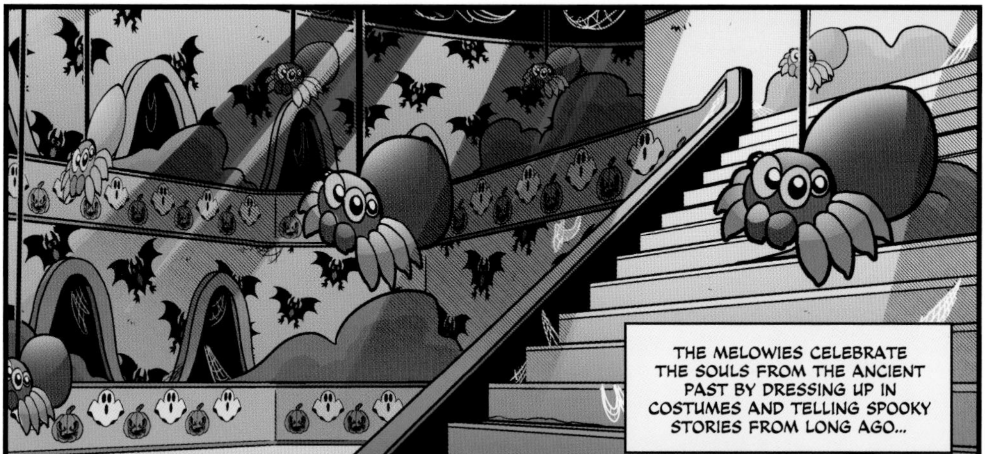
THE MELOWIES CELEBRATE THE SOULS FROM THE ANCIENT PAST BY DRESSING UP IN COSTUMES AND TELLING SPOOKY STORIES FROM LONG AGO...

CORTNEY FAYE POWELL, WRITER, AND RYAN JAMPOLE, ARTIST.

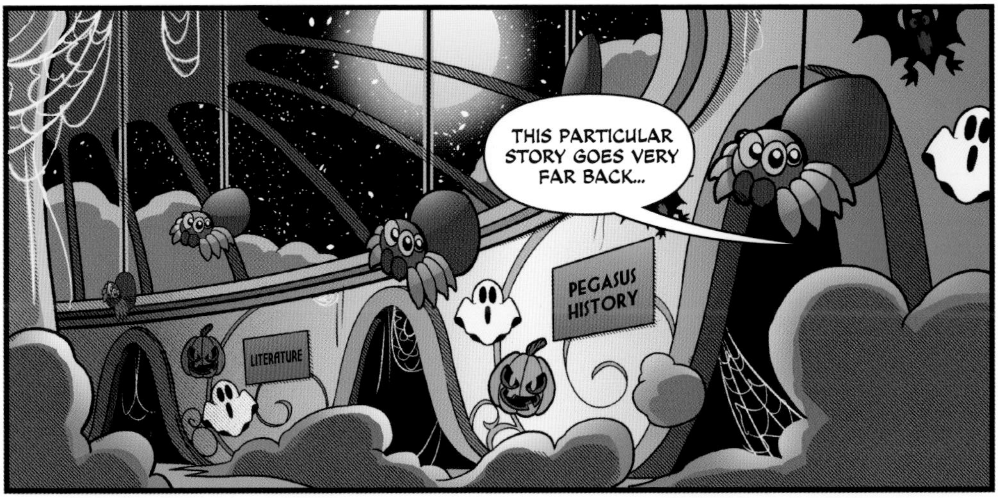
THIS PARTICULAR STORY GOES VERY FAR BACK...
PEGASUS HISTORY
LITERATURE

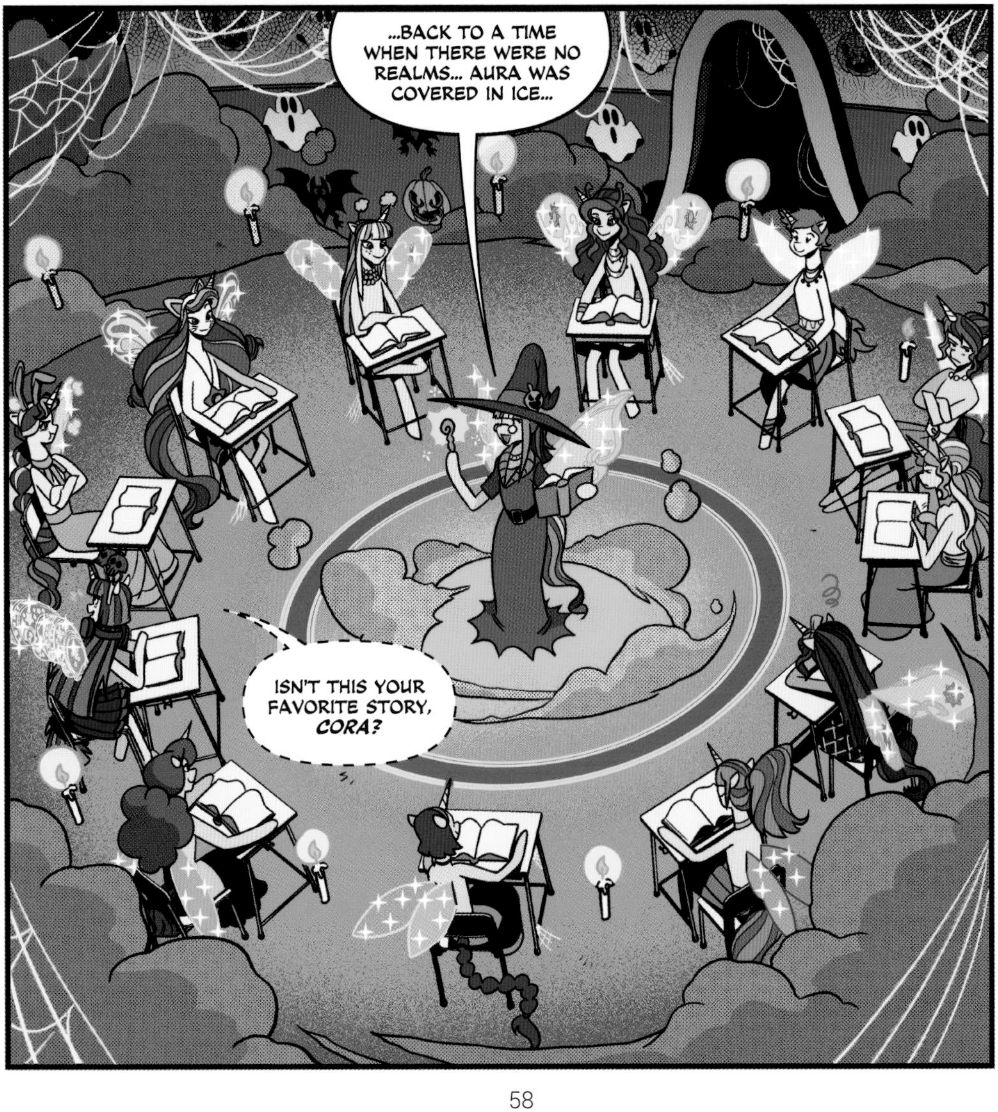
...BACK TO A TIME WHEN THERE WERE NO REALMS... AURA WAS COVERED IN ICE...
ISN'T THIS YOUR FAVORITE STORY, *CORA?*

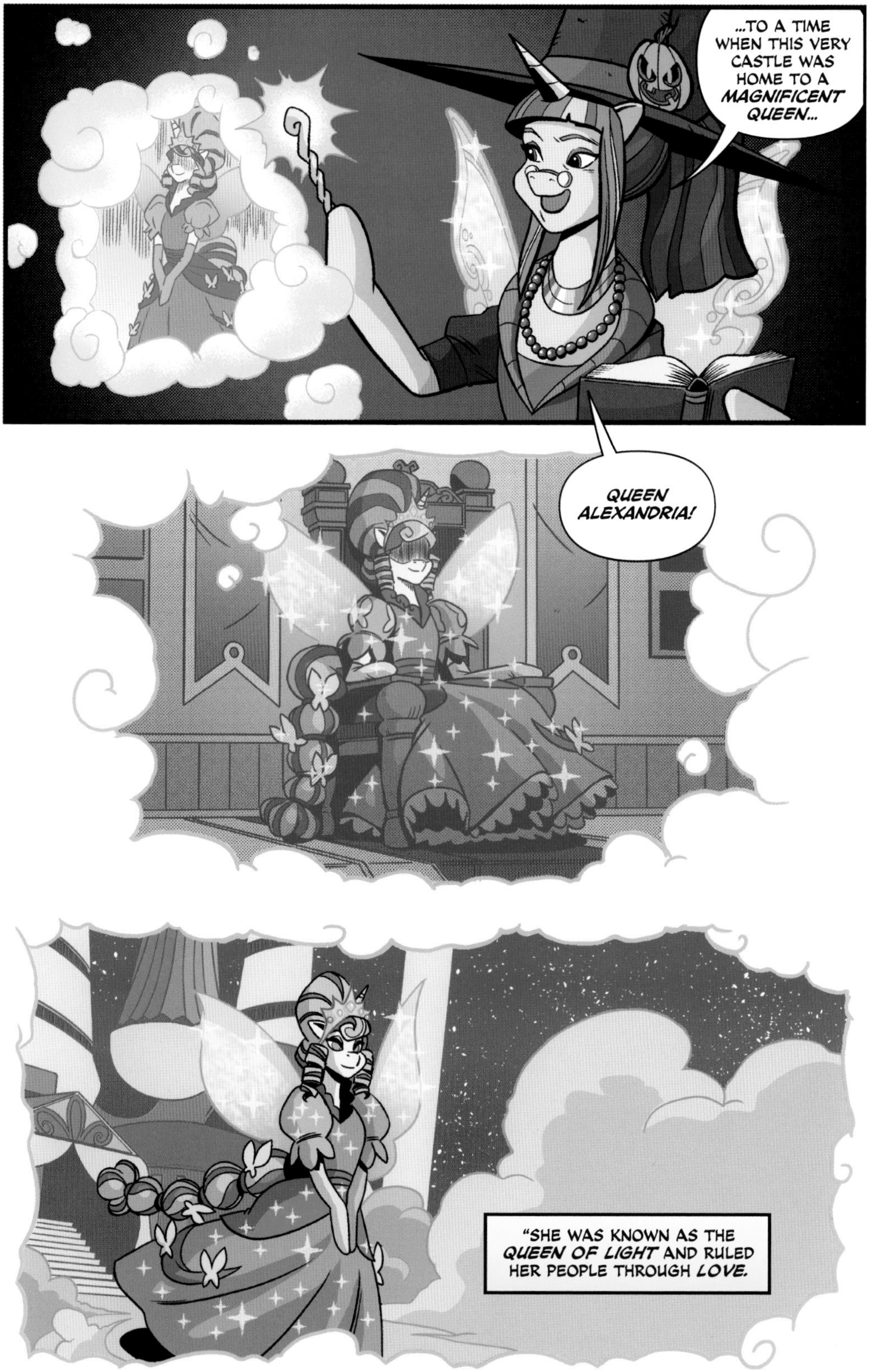
...TO A TIME WHEN THIS VERY CASTLE WAS HOME TO A *MAGNIFICENT QUEEN...*
QUEEN ALEXANDRIA!
"SHE WAS KNOWN AS THE *QUEEN OF LIGHT* AND RULED HER PEOPLE THROUGH *LOVE.*

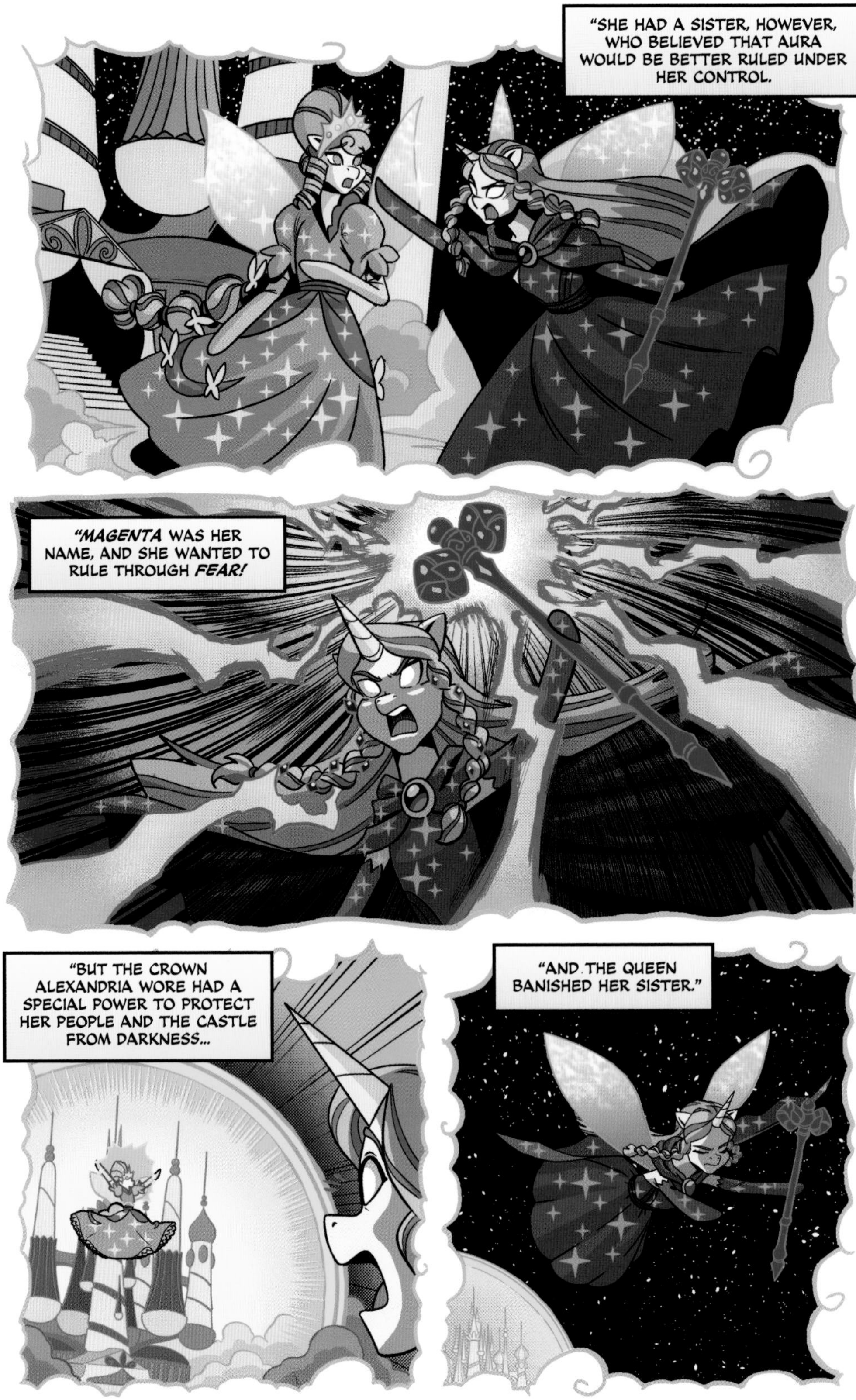
"SHE HAD A SISTER, HOWEVER, WHO BELIEVED THAT AURA WOULD BE BETTER RULED UNDER HER CONTROL.
"*MAGENTA* WAS HER NAME, AND SHE WANTED TO RULE THROUGH *FEAR!*
"BUT THE CROWN ALEXANDRIA WORE HAD A SPECIAL POWER TO PROTECT HER PEOPLE AND THE CASTLE FROM DARKNESS...
"AND THE QUEEN BANISHED HER SISTER."

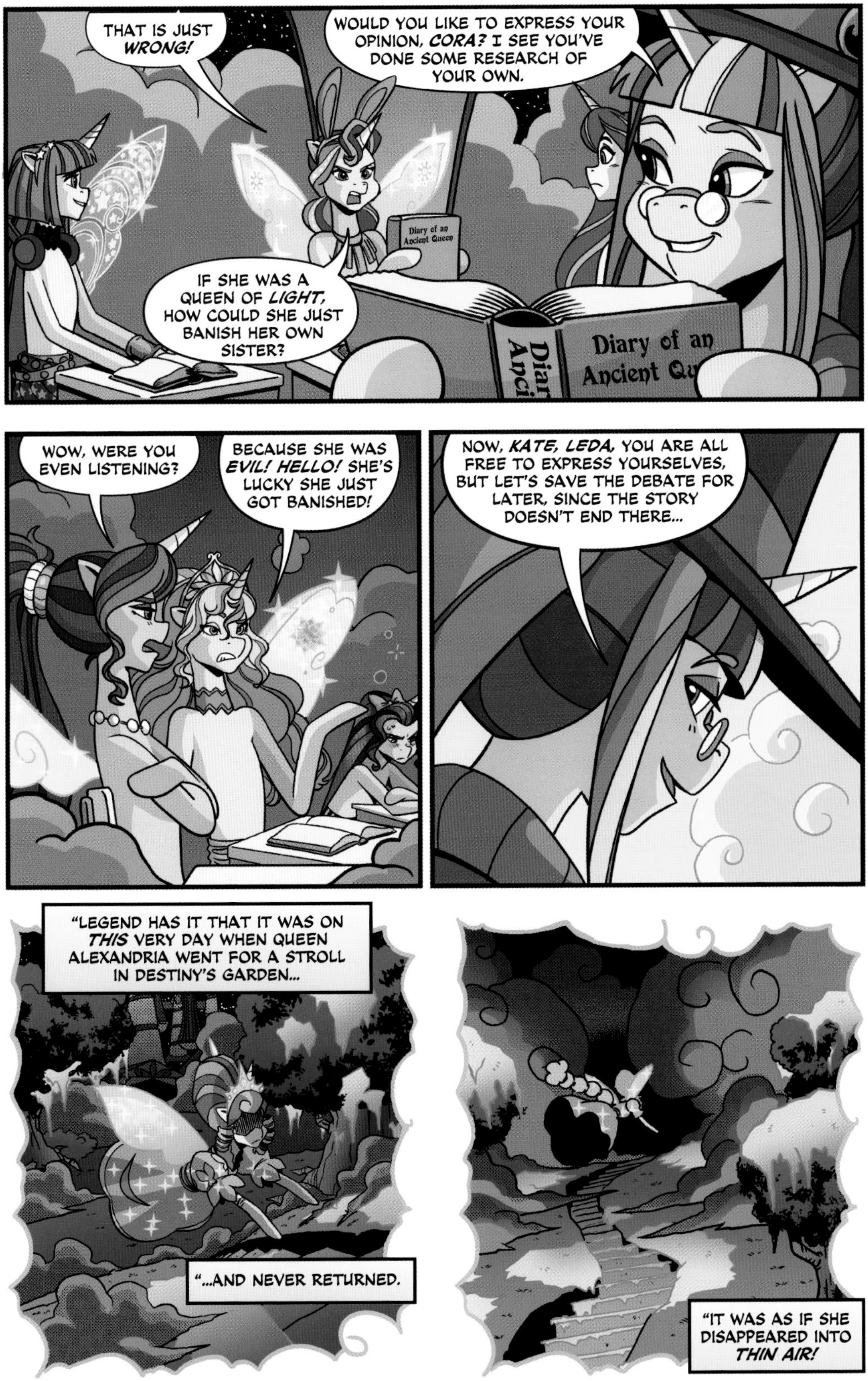
THAT IS JUST *WRONG!*
WOULD YOU LIKE TO EXPRESS YOUR OPINION, *CORA?* I SEE YOU'VE DONE SOME RESEARCH OF YOUR OWN.
Diary of an Ancient Queen
IF SHE WAS A QUEEN OF *LIGHT,* HOW COULD SHE JUST BANISH HER OWN SISTER?
WOW, WERE YOU EVEN LISTENING?
BECAUSE SHE WAS *EVIL! HELLO!* SHE'S LUCKY SHE JUST GOT BANISHED!
NOW, *KATE, LEDA,* YOU ARE ALL FREE TO EXPRESS YOURSELVES, BUT LET'S SAVE THE DEBATE FOR LATER, SINCE THE STORY DOESN'T END THERE...
"LEGEND HAS IT THAT IT WAS ON *THIS* VERY DAY WHEN QUEEN ALEXANDRIA WENT FOR A STROLL IN DESTINY'S GARDEN...
"...AND NEVER RETURNED.
"IT WAS AS IF SHE DISAPPEARED INTO *THIN AIR!*

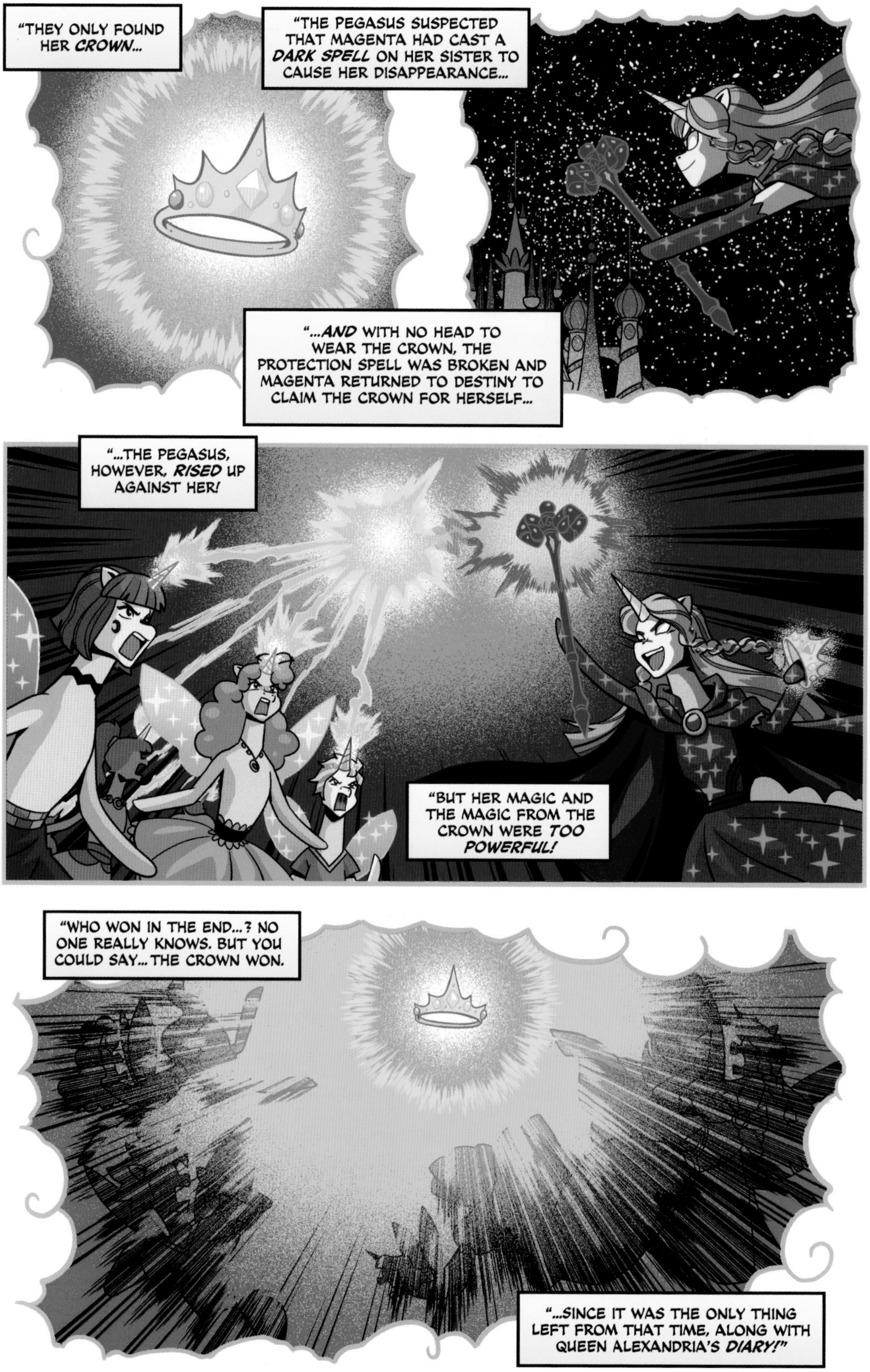
"THEY ONLY FOUND HER *CROWN*...
"THE PEGASUS SUSPECTED THAT MAGENTA HAD CAST A *DARK SPELL* ON HER SISTER TO CAUSE HER DISAPPEARANCE...
"...*AND* WITH NO HEAD TO WEAR THE CROWN, THE PROTECTION SPELL WAS BROKEN AND MAGENTA RETURNED TO DESTINY TO CLAIM THE CROWN FOR HERSELF...
"...THE PEGASUS, HOWEVER, *RISED* UP AGAINST HER!
"BUT HER MAGIC AND THE MAGIC FROM THE CROWN WERE *TOO POWERFUL!*
"WHO WON IN THE END...? NO ONE REALLY KNOWS. BUT YOU COULD SAY... THE CROWN WON.
"...SINCE IT WAS THE ONLY THING LEFT FROM THAT TIME, ALONG WITH QUEEN ALEXANDRIA'S *DIARY!*"

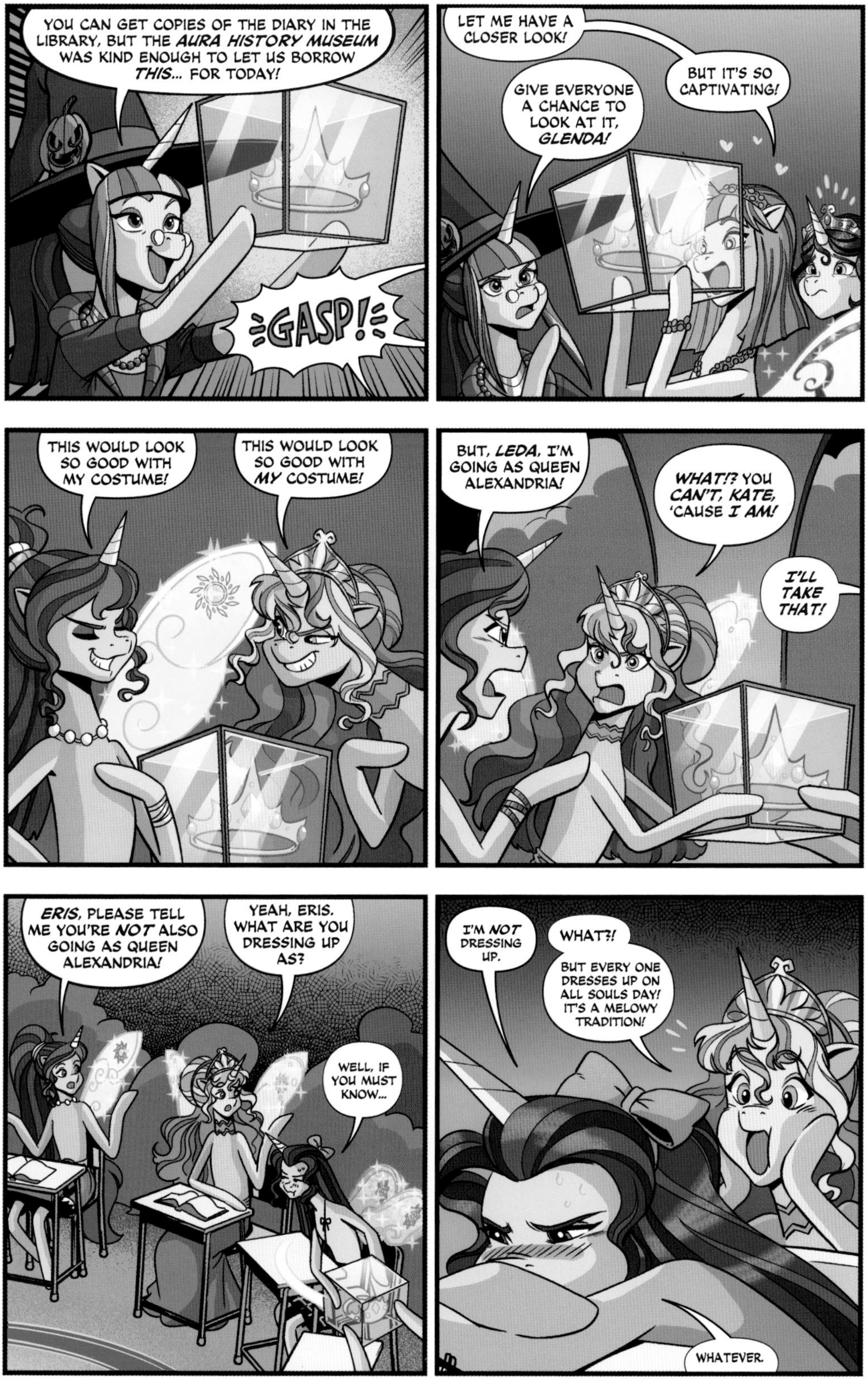
YOU CAN GET COPIES OF THE DIARY IN THE LIBRARY, BUT THE AURA HISTORY MUSEUM WAS KIND ENOUGH TO LET US BORROW THIS... FOR TODAY!
GASP!
LET ME HAVE A CLOSER LOOK!
GIVE EVERYONE A CHANCE TO LOOK AT IT, GLENDA!
BUT IT'S SO CAPTIVATING!
THIS WOULD LOOK SO GOOD WITH MY COSTUME!
THIS WOULD LOOK SO GOOD WITH MY COSTUME!
BUT, LEDA, I'M GOING AS QUEEN ALEXANDRIA!
WHAT!? YOU CAN'T, KATE, 'CAUSE I AM!
I'LL TAKE THAT!
ERIS, PLEASE TELL ME YOU'RE NOT ALSO GOING AS QUEEN ALEXANDRIA!
YEAH, ERIS. WHAT ARE YOU DRESSING UP AS?
WELL, IF YOU MUST KNOW...
I'M NOT DRESSING UP.
WHAT?!
BUT EVERY ONE DRESSES UP ON ALL SOULS DAY! IT'S A MELOWY TRADITION!
WHATEVER.

Get the full story in MELOWY #5 "Meloween," available now at booksellers and libraries everywhere!

Geronimo Stilton

GRAPHIC NOVELS AVAILABLE FROM PAPERCUTZ

#1
"The Discovery
of America"

#2
"The Secret
of the Sphinx"

#3
"The Coliseum
Con"

#4
"Following the
Trail of Marco Polo"

#5
"The Great
Ice Age"

#6
"Who Stole
The Mona Lisa?"

#7
"Dinosaurs
in Action"

#8
"Play It Again,
Mozart!"

#9
"The Weird
Book Machine"

#10
"Geronimo Stilton
Saves the Olympics"

#11
"We'll Always
Have Paris"

#12
"The First Samurai"

#13
"The Fastest Train
in the West"

#14
"The First Mouse
on the Moon"

#15
"All for Stilton,
Stilton for All!"

#16
"Lights, Camera,
Stilton!"

#17
"The Mystery of the
Pirate Ship"

#18
"First to the Last Place
on Earth"

#19
"Lost in Translation"

GERONIMO STILTON
3 in 1 #1

GERONIMO STILTON
3 in 1 #2

GERONIMO STILTON
3 in 1 #3

GERONIMO STILTON
3 in 1 #4

GERONIMO STILTON
3 in 1 #5

...ALSO AVAILABLE
WHEREVER E-BOOKS
ARE SOLD!

See more at
papercutz.com

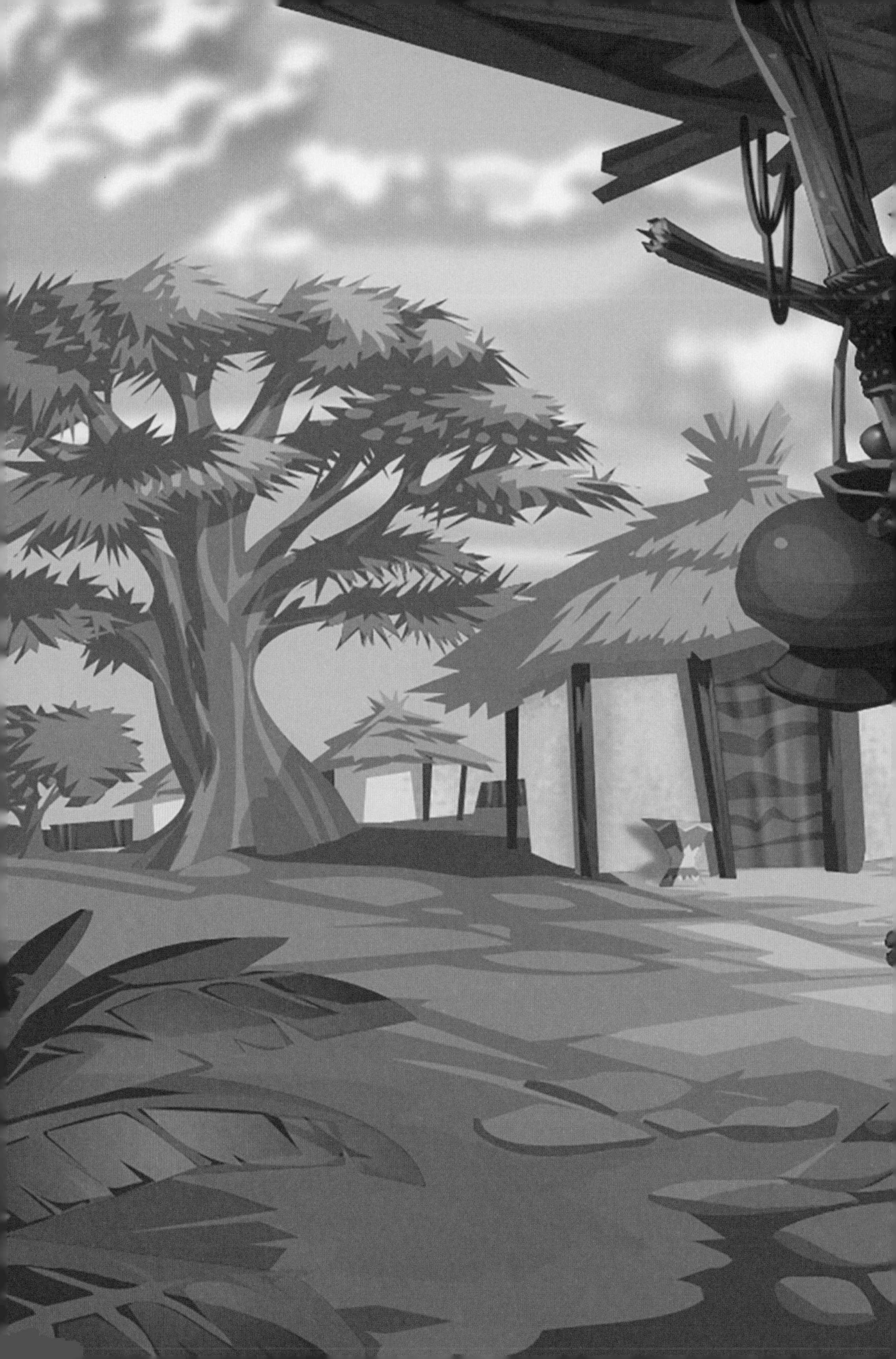